Dear Reader,

Home, family, community and love. These are the values we cherish most in our lives—the ideals that ground us, comfort us, move us. They certainly provide the perfect inspiration around which to build a romance collection that will touch the heart.

And so we are thrilled to have the opportunity to introduce you to the Harlequin Heartwarming collection. Each of these special stories is a wholesome, heartfelt romance imbued with the traditional values so important to you. They are books you can share proudly with friends and family. And the authors featured in this collection are some of the most talented storytellers writing today, including favorites such as Laura Abbot, Roz Denny Fox, Jillian Hart and Irene Hannon. We've selected these stories especially for you based on their overriding qualities of emotion and tenderness, and they center around your favorite themes—children, weddings, second chances, the reunion of families, the quest to find a true home and, of course, sweet romance.

So curl up in your favorite chair, relax and prepare for a heartwarming reading experience!

Sincerely,

The Editors

D0324740

JILLIAN HART

grew up on her family's homestead, where she helped raise cattle, rode horses and scribbled stories in her spare time. After earning her English degree from Whitman College, she worked in travel and advertising before selling her first novel. When Jillian isn't working on her next story, she can be found puttering in her rose garden, curled up with a good book or spending quiet evenings at home with her family.

HARLEQUIN HEARTWARMING

Jillian Hart

Gifts from the Heart

TORONTO NEW YORK LONDON
AMSTERDAM PARIS SYDNEY HAMBURG
STOCKHOLM ATHENS TOKYO MILAN MADRID
PRAGUE WARSAW BUDAPEST AUCKLAND

Recycling programs
for this product may
not exist in your area.

ISBN-13: 978-0-373-36416-9

GIFTS FROM THE HEART

Copyright © 2011 by Jill Strickler

Originally published as THE SWEETEST GIFT © 2004 by Jill Strickler

Gifts from the Heart

To my Jessie

Chapter One

"Sister dearest, you look as though you need a café mocha with extra whipped cream."

"Boy, do I." Kirby McKaslin sagged against the coffee shop's counter. "Could you make it a double?"

"Gladly." Older sister Karen's diamond wedding ring glittered in the overhead lights as she began working the espresso machine. "Come around and help yourself to the leftover cookies. Gramma made chocolate chocolate-chip—"

"Say no more." Kirby dropped her purse on the counter and swung around the corner. Gramma's soft, chewy chocolate cookies were heaven on earth. There were only two left in the display case and she grabbed both of them.

"What about the job?" Karen set the double mocha with a froth of whipped cream on the counter, her voice affectionate and understanding, as always.

Kirby couldn't hide her smile a second longer. "I got it. I'm the new nurse practitioner at the Three Forks Clinic. I start in two weeks."

"Kirby! That's fantastic!" Karen circled the edge of the counter, arms wide. "I'm so proud of my little sister."

"It's too good to be true. My very own clinic. I'm totally in charge, and I know I'm going to love it." Kirby stepped into her sister's hug. "I'm going to get my own patients. I still can't believe it."

"I can. I've had faith in you all along."

There was nothing like a big sister. Kirby gave Karen an extra-long hug, careful of the growing tummy beneath her loose T-shirt. Married and expecting, with a new house and a booming business, Karen had it all.

Kirby was glad for her, but, well, it would be great if that kind of future was ahead for her, too. Not that there were any prospects, but you never knew when a handsome stranger with a loving heart would walk into your life and complete it, right?

She felt optimistic as she sipped melting whipped cream and hot, rich mocha. Things were finally working out in her life. She felt great. As she pushed through the shop's front door and burst onto the sidewalk she couldn't remember being this happy in a long time.

She'd head home. Let her dog out for a run. Maybe treat them both to their favorite drive-through hamburgers…

"Kendra!" a woman shouted out from beneath the awning across the street. "Kendra!"

Kirby didn't need to look up from the sunshine falling on the concrete in front of her to know her excellent mood was about to take a nosedive. Doom was the cheerful former cheerleader across the street, holding tight to her newborn with one hand and waving frantically with the other.

"Kendra, I'm so relieved I finally found you." Janice Bemis turned on her charm. "What luck! I've been looking for you. You just *have* to join the class reunion committee."

"I'm not interested, Janice. And it's Kirby, not Kendra." Someone she'd gone to school with since kindergarten ought to know that sort of thing. That was the problem with being the plainest girl in the family—and the middle girl. No one could remember which one she was.

"Goodness, I'm so sorry."

"That's all right." She was used to it. She dug her keys out of her pocket with her free hand, heading straight to her car.

"I'll give you a call and we'll talk!" Janice promised with die-hard cheerfulness.

Right, and I have caller ID. Kirby settled on the seat of her little red sedan and let the hot, sweet double mocha work its magic. As soon as enough chocolate was in her bloodstream, she started feeling better again.

The last time I volunteered on a committee with you, Janice Appleton Bemis, you stole the boy I was interested in and humiliated me in front of half the student body. Get some-one else for your committee. That's what she should have said. Sure, easy to think of all those words *now,* when she was halfway down Railroad Street.

She wasn't going to let Janice ruin her mood. No way. This was the best day Kirby had had in ages—finally a better-paying job, which meant she got to keep the house she'd bought and couldn't *quite* afford.

If that wasn't good news enough, her loud

and noisy next-door neighbor had been evicted yesterday.

Relief sighed through her. Another blissful night of peaceful and uninterrupted sleep was ahead of her tonight. That would make two nights in a row. It sounded like heaven.

If she ever needed confirmation that dreams came true, this was it.

Until she pulled down her street and spotted the strange pickup parked in her next-door neighbor's driveway. Her happiness began to ebb. Surely Ruth Gardner, the landlord, hadn't found a new renter already.

No, probably not. It's only a repairman, she told herself. There's no way someone else could have moved in already. And Ruth had promised she'd find a renter more suitable to the neighborhood.

That's *definitely* a repairman, Kirby decided as she slowed down, fighting the seat belt to twist around for a better look. It certainly wasn't someone moving in, not with the ladder and a big box of tools in the back of the pickup.

Just how many repairs would the house need? How soon before it would be rented? After six months of torment putting up with noise, she had a right to be curious.

Who was fixing the house? Was it a general contractor, meaning the job would take a long time? Or a handyman come to do minor repairs?

Ooh, there he was. The workman loped down the front steps and into sight. He was a dark-haired man, probably six feet tall with wide shoulders and lanky rather than bulky build. He wore a red baseball cap and a gray T-shirt and jeans. A tool belt hugged his lean hips. That was all she saw before she pulled into her driveway and the hedges separating the properties hid him from her sight.

Hmm... Whether he was there for major repairs or minor, he was definitely handsome. Not that handsome men paid her any attention, let's face it—she'd never had that kind of luck. But it never hurt a girl to appreciate the pleasing form of a hardworking man.

Especially a girl who wanted a husband to call her own. But not just any man—the right one. That man was turning out to be harder to find than she'd ever dreamed.

Kirby killed the engine and set the parking brake. Her keys tinkled merrily as she climbed from the car, careful not to spill her steaming mocha. The tepid breezes whipped her dark blond hair into her face, and out of habit she folded the long strands behind her ear as she headed up the walk.

Who would her ideal next-door neighbor be? How about as handsome as the workman next door? And he'd be quiet and sedate, too. Polite. Hardworking. Kind.

Oh, and wonderful in every way. Someone exactly the opposite from the single, wild-haired guy who'd just moved out and who'd played his bass guitar in his garage night after night from midnight until four in the morning.

No, her ideal man would be soft-spoken and considerate and looking for his true love. Of course, he'd take one look at her and fall instantly in love—

"Howdy." A bold male voice came out of nowhere.

Kirby yelped and a bubble of foam popped up through the drink hole in the plastic cover, scorching her hand. A suspicious rustling had her turning toward the hedge along the property line.

A man climbed through the foliage like James Bond on a mission.

Or like a prisoner on a jailbreak.

Evergreen needles dusted his dark, short hair. Yep, it was the workman from next door.

He was more powerful looking up close. Developed muscles corded his lean, rock-solid arms. He looked intimidating as he straightened to his full height, probably a few inches over six foot, on the lawn in front of her.

Why was he coming through the shrubs instead of walking around on the sidewalk like a normal person?

"I scared you," he said, apparently not shy at all, as he dusted bits of green hedge off his gray shirt.

Say something. Kirby took a breath, trying fruitlessly to get past the shyness that always haunted her.

"I'm sorry. I guess you're not used to men bursting through your hedges."

"Most people use the sidewalk. There are fewer branches to trip over." Oh, that was brilliant, Kirby.

"I'm a unique sort of guy. I never take the easy route. My friends call me Sam."

Friends? "Then what do your enemies call you?"

"Deadly with an M-16." His rugged face was as unforgiving as stone.

Adrenaline kicked up in her blood. Okay, time to run into the house and lock the door. It wouldn't hurt to be on the other side of the dead bolt. A man who mentioned a gun had to be dangerous, right?

"I used to be in the military."

Okay, so *now* he tells her, after scaring her to death. Who is this guy? she wondered. Kirby took a few more deep breaths, wiped her hand off on her slacks and studied him. He didn't look dangerous at all with the sunlight spilling over him and his hands jammed harmlessly into his front pockets.

What an imagination she had. "Thanks for clarifying that. For a minute there, I thought you might be a convict on the loose."

"Nope, just a man come to fix the plumbing next door." One corner of his mouth crooked in the attempt at a grin, but it was a failed attempt. His face seemed too hard for a smile. "Sorry, I guess I scared you. Didn't mean to."

"Really? Here's a hint. Next time you introduce yourself to a woman, don't mention an assault weapon."

He winced. "I was kidding about that. My buddies call me the comedian."

Comedian? He looked dead serious. As if there wasn't one thing amusing about him. But he was a big man and in fantastic shape, and so she wasn't going to argue. If he thought he was funny, then she was happy to let him think that.

At least her heart rate was almost back to normal. "Fine, well, I'm going to go in now. Nice meeting you..." Whatever your name is.

"Sam."

"What?" Her pulse rocketed up a notch.

"Sam Gardner." His rock-hard brown gaze pinned hers. "Guess I should have introduced myself properly. So a woman alone and as skittish as you would feel comfortable."

She'd be offended by his tone, except that there was a glimmer of humor in his eyes. Oh, she knew about men like him. Too handsome for his own good, and he knew it, too.

Shouldn't he be next door repairing the plumbing? Why was he bugging her?

He arched his brow, and on his granite face it was more of a demand than a question. "I've told you my name. So it'd be polite if you told me yours."

"I never said I was polite."

"Darlin', you have it written all over that peaches-and-cream complexion of yours." A hint of a smile played on his mouth. "Go ahead. You can say it. My name is...?"

"Kirby. Is there some reason you climbed through my hedge?"

"There sure is. I only crash through hedges for a good cause. I'm here because I'm in trouble."

"Oh, I see." Of course that's why he was here. Why he was laying on the charm. He wanted something. "Let me guess. You need to use my phone to make a long-distance emergency call."

"Nope, but are you offering? I *could* think of someone to call long distance."

"No."

What was he doing? Sam Gardner knew better than to tease a pretty young woman, especially one so seemingly good and innocent, because he'd learned from experience. No good could come from it. Hugging a nestful of rattlers would be less hazardous.

That's why he did it. He saw the way she'd looked him up and down as potential marriage material. Single women of a certain age had that common habit, and he had to make it clear. He was *not* a candidate for holy matrimony. The question was, did she get the hint?

Her bow-shaped mouth drew down. Oh, yeah, she was expecting the worst from him.

"You want me to fix you a sandwich? Run to the hardware store for you? Lend you money? My grandmother warned me about men like you."

"Good guys, you mean?"

Her delicate brows arched above her perfect, blue-sky eyes. He'd managed to offend her pretty well.

Good. Mission complete.

"No, men who try to offend women on *purpose*."

Ooh...*busted*. He'd have to watch this one. She was smarter than she looked. "You can't blame a guy for trying to make a memorable impression."

"Memorable? You would have been better off wearing a ski mask and asking for all my money. I'd be more relaxed around you."

"I had you believing that for a few minutes. C'mon, I saw that look on your face when you dashed for the door."

"I did not dash."

"You were ready to."

"Maybe, but you do look like a man who can't be trusted." She lit up as she said that. And she may as well have plastered "single and looking" on her forehead in neon-red ink.

He hadn't been promoted as fast as he had in the armed forces without being dead-on when it came to reading people and knowing what they were capable of. And pretty blond women of a certain age without a diamond on their left ring finger wanted only one thing.

Yep, he'd be wary of her. Friendly, but wary.

"So, are you gonna help me out or not?"

"I'll take it under consideration."

While she thought about it, she took a sip of her coffee—he could smell the chocolate and caffeine from four paces away. That frilly drink probably had extra whipped cream and those chocolate candy sprinkle things, too.

She eyed him over the top of the pastel-pink straws she was daintily sipping from. Was she still trying to figure out if he was suitable marriage material? Or had he convinced her that he wasn't?

"I can't believe you conned Mrs. Gardner into hiring you. She isn't paying you to stand on my walkway talking to me."

"She's not paying me. I'm fixing her house out of the kindness of my own good heart."

"Excuse me, but you don't look the type."

pearances can be deceiving."

"Let me get this straight. You're fixing the plumbing next door for free?"

"Hey, don't look so surprised. I know I don't look like those *GQ* kind of men or the suit-and-tie-wearing office types who say please and thank you. I don't have 'feelings.' But I'm not a jerk out to profit off an old lady on a fixed income. I'm Ruth's nephew."

Kirby's rosebud mouth dropped open in surprise. "Her nephew? *You?*"

"That's an affirmative."

She stared at him. "Ruth Gardner is petite and blond, and you look like James Bond gone bad. Are you sure you're related to her?"

James Bond, huh? He liked that. "Yep. She married my dad's brother. He passed last year. I came for the funeral and realized how alone Ruth was. No children of her own, and so she'd always done her best to spoil me when I was growing up. I figured I might move here and keep an eye on her. She's the only family I've got."

Kirby's blue eyes warmed a notch as she studied him again. This time with a much higher regard. "Ruth's a very nice lady. I'm sure she's relieved you're helping her out with this house. She had nothing but problems with the last renters."

"Yep, but I came and evicted them. No more problems."

"I can't tell you how much I appreciate that. You'll find a nice quiet couple or a young family, maybe. Responsible people to rent, right?"

There she went, being too friendly again. He'd gone too far. He didn't think of himself as a man with natural charm. In fact, he *tried* to scare away marriage-seeking women on purpose. Looked as if he'd better try harder.

"So, what about that favor? I had to shut off the water to the house. Trouble is, I need to flush a pipe, and I can't turn on the main valve. Would you let me use your garden hose for about five minutes?"

"Five minutes, not six?"

"How about five and a half?"

"Deal. The hose is in the back. Just go through the side gate." Soft humor sparkled in those pretty blue eyes of hers.

Not that he was dazzled in the least by her pretty blue eyes. He was a disciplined man, and he knew enough about women to know he'd better stop noticing how lovely she was. The girl-next-door type was always the same.

Always. He ought to know, since he'd married one, and what a disaster that had been.

Don't think about it, man. Sam forced the memories away even before they could bounce off the titanium shield around his heart. He was well protected. Self-controlled. He wasn't going to think that because Kirby was nice, she would be any different deep down when times got tough. Because she wouldn't be.

Keep your distance, Gardner. That would be the wisest course. He hadn't survived some of the toughest battles in recent military history only to let another woman take him down. He knew how to get out of disasters alive and when to avoid them entirely.

He knew exactly how love could break a man, and what a nice, sweet-looking woman could do to his soul.

He was here for a reason, nothing more. "Is the gate locked?"

"No." She flicked a golden strand of hair behind her slim shoulder, her brows furrowed beneath her wispy, windblown bangs, as if she were trying to look deep inside him.

Good luck. He didn't let anyone close, most of all a lovely woman like her with a heart-shaped face, a creamy clear complexion and a few freckles scattered across the bridge of her nose. Freckles she tried to hide with a light coat of makeup. Not that he was noticing. He wasn't. Really.

Her lips were bare of lipstick or of that shiny-looking stuff women wore on those makeup commercials. Her mouth was softly shaped and kind, as if she smiled. *A lot.*

Yep, she was sure going to be trouble. Trouble because he liked her on sight. And hated that he did. "There's a few boards missing off the top of the fence I need to fix, but I'm gonna need access to your yard to do it. Do you mind?"

"No, but that's half of my fence, too, and I should pay you."

"Seeing as you're willing to compensate me, I'd sure appreciate a tall glass of iced tea."

"Fine. Iced tea it is. But only half a glass up front," she called over her shoulder as she unlocked her front door. "You'll get the rest when the job's finished."

"What?"

"Isn't that the standard business practice? When I had my new roof put on, it was half payment up front. The rest on completion of a satisfactory job."

He laughed. He couldn't help it. "Lady, that's no way to treat your new neighbor."

Chapter Two

Neighbor? Kirby whirled around. This couldn't be true.

"Yep. Surprised you, did I? You didn't think I'd be your new next-door neighbor. Your new next-door nightmare."

The keys tumbled from her fingers and hit the front step with a terrible, final clink as if to say, "Disaster."

She rescued her keys from the ground, heart pounding and her mind spinning. No, she couldn't have heard him right. There was no possible way. Ruth had made promises. Ruth was a trustworthy, dependable woman. Ruth wouldn't have lied or broken her word. *Next time I'll find a decent, quiet, responsible neighbor,* she'd said.

This man looked anything but quiet and

responsible. He looked as if a squad of Special Forces commandos might come by at any moment and recruit him.

"You're kidding, right?"

"Nope. I bought furniture this morning. It's gonna be delivered tomorrow between ten and noon." He wedged his hands in his jeans pockets, widening his stance. His chest was impressively broad and strong looking.

Not that she should be noticing. "You can't be my new neighbor. I mean, the house isn't even up for rent yet. I know, because I just talked to Ruth yesterday."

"You didn't speak with her today, did you? Or you'd have all the latest details."

Doom. Kirby could feel a dark cloud settle around her like midnight fog.

What had Mrs. Gardner promised? *That's a mistake I won't repeat again, dear—you have my word on that. No more bachelors in my rental house. I know there are discrimination laws, but those single men can sure be trouble....*

Sam Gardner looked like a single man to her, nephew or not, since no wedding ring marked the fourth finger of his left hand.

Or was he the kind of married man who didn't wear a ring? That was even worse!

He paced closer. "You suddenly don't look very happy. You don't approve?"

"I'm wary because I've had my fair share of neighbor disasters."

"Like fires?"

"Not fires. Weekend parties and night-long drum practice sessions in the garage." Which she hadn't been able to sleep through.

Please, at least let him be married. Stable. Did she dare hope that he was very busy being a plumber during the day so he had to sleep at night? "Will you be inviting over large numbers of people and playing heavy metal music extremely loud after midnight?"

"Probably. The good news is that I won't be living alone for much longer. My rock-band buddies will be moving in shortly." One dark brow quirked. "Is that what you mean by neighbor disasters?"

She saw the next six months of peaceful nights' sleeping vanish before her eyes. "Yes, that's exactly what I mean."

Catastrophe. There was no other word for it. And this was Mrs. Gardner's relative. There was no way she'd evict her own nephew.

"I throw wild parties at least three times a week. That's why I got booted out from my last five apartments." He winked at her. "Did that answer your question?"

He was teasing her. Great. She'd been hoping for a nice responsible neighbor and what did she get? A comedian. He'd been teasing her all along.

She didn't *want* to like him. The only reason a handsome man like him paid any attention to a girl like her was that they wanted something. Wasn't that the way it was? She was ordinary looking, nothing special, and that was okay, because it just showed this man was not her Mr. Right.

Her true love would see past her plainness and see her. And he'd love her, shortcomings and failures and strengths. That's the way love should be.

She unlocked her second lock as her little dog barked through the wooden door. "Oh, about the hose. Please don't forget to coil it up when you're through."

"I'll leave it the way I found it. Don't worry. I might be loud and inconsiderate when I'm playing my drums all night, but I'm careful with garden hoses."

Why was she laughing? She shouldn't be encouraging him. She snatched her mail from the slim black box next to the front door. She wasn't even going to look at the bills that had come. She had bigger problems. Her new neighbor. So he wasn't what she'd hoped for. He wasn't going to be a problem, right?

Maybe she wasn't seeing the whole picture. Maybe he'd taken off his wedding ring when he worked so he wouldn't catch it on a pipe or something. That meant there was a chance he could be married and responsible.

He didn't look responsible, but still, a girl had to have hope. "Will your wife be joining you?"

"No, no wife. No woman can put up with all the groupies from my band."

"I can't believe Mrs. Gardner is letting a man like you stay in her house."

"There's this nondiscrimination law. She had to let me in or I threatened to sue." Dimples cut into his cheeks as he tunneled his hands into the front pockets of his jeans, standing strong and at ease, like a man always in charge. "Don't worry, I'll be a good neighbor. I won't throw parties and don't play loud music. I'm usually working."

"Working." She should have guessed it by the hard, lean look of him. "Don't tell me you're one of those workaholic types."

"Yes, but it's not my fault. It's genetic. I

tried a support group for a while, but it cut into my work time."

"I suppose it's a competitive, stressful calling, being a plumber. Nighttime leaking pipes, early-morning bathtub backups and emergency pipe unclogging."

"Are you mocking me?" That seemed to make those troublesome glints in his eyes shine more brightly. "Sure, go ahead and make me angry. I may have to go let off steam. Did I mention I play drums? Yep. I plan to set up in the garage. Will that bother you at night?"

He flashed her a grin before padding soundlessly away. He moved like a well-trained athlete, like a man comfortable with his power. Not married, huh?

She was a woman. She couldn't help noticing the wide, capable cut of his shoulders beneath the plain gray T-shirt. Or his long legs encased in denim as he disappeared around the corner of her house.

Not that she was interested. She wanted a nice marrying man. He looked like anything but.

"Best get the tea steeping, because I'm a fast worker," he called from the side yard, out of sight.

The side gate of the fence squealed open and then snapped shut.

He might not be Mr. Right, but he was funny. Heroes in the movies weren't this good-looking.

Her dog started barking an enthusiastic greeting through the door. Kirby banned all thoughts of Sam Gardner from her head and turned the old brass knob.

The instant she opened the door, the little spaniel leaped at her knees, panting happily. Kirby knelt to hug the wiggling creature. There was nothing like being welcomed home. And until she had a family of her own, she was blessed with this little animal that was always so glad to see her.

"C'mon, Jessie. Let's get you outside." Kirby's problems felt far away as she set down her purse and followed her best friend through the house. The little blond dog, nothing but fluff, curls and long ears, dashed ahead, leading the way.

"Did you have a good day guarding the house?" Kirby talked to fill the silence that was broken only by the occasional creak of the wood floorboards and the tap of her heels. "I know, it's a tough job, but you did well. Yes, you did."

The dog panted happily, already at the back door, sitting politely and gazing at the doorknob.

There he was! Sam Gardner. Kirby froze at the sight of him, then took one step back away from the window. Staying out of his sight, she watched him through the sun-streaked glass. Looking like a rodeo hero, he slung the coiled green hose into the air like a lasso. It unfurled as it sailed over the top of the fence and into his backyard.

Sam Gardner met only one of her criteria. He was attractive. She watched his toned muscles ripple beneath his T-shirt as he adjusted the hose over the top of the board fence and stalked out of sight.

Too bad. She'd be willing to settle for him if he met even one more of her criteria.

A second later, she could hear the sound of water running. "What do you think, Jess?"

The dog didn't bother to bark. She looked at the doorknob expectantly.

"Some watchdog you are. You're too friendly. You didn't even snarl when he was in the backyard."

The dog gazed up at her happily, long silky ears flopping, pink tongue lolling.

"I know, you're a fierce one." Kirby patted

the dog's soft round head, laughing because she couldn't imagine her sweet-hearted dog hurting anyone.

She couldn't imagine Sam Gardner running from anyone or anything. He had that tough, dangerous look about him. The one that made a girl's pulse skyrocket. Even an average and ordinary girl like her.

There he was again. She could see him on the other side of the fence, in his yard, tugging the hose in a competent, expert way that said he could handle anything. Shocks of dark hair tumbled over his brow as he worked, and the sunshine flitted over him like grace.

He's probably not responsible, not nice, not considerate and hardworking, she told herself, as if that were any consolation. Except that didn't ring true.

The dog scratched at the door.

Had she drifted off again? Yep, she was always doing that. Kirby turned the knob and opened the door. Maybe she'd go out with the dog and make sure Sam had shut the side gate. He didn't look like the responsible type—

A shadow leaped toward her. Big. Dark. Threatening. She fell back against the door, from calm to terrified in a millisecond. She tried to scream.

Couldn't.

The shadow became an enormous dog hurtling toward her. Its powerful jaw opened to reveal enormous sharp teeth. He leaped through the open door and planted his huge muddy paws on her shoulders. Bright, happy brown eyes smiled at her. A wide, wet tongue swiped across her chin in a friendly hello.

"I guess you're not too dangerous." Kirby wiped her face with her sleeve. "Down."

Pleased with himself, the dog dropped to all fours, glad to sniff noses with the little blond spaniel dancing around him in greeting.

That was one enormous dog. He was at least midthigh high, with a neat, short black-and-brown coat. He paraded into her kitchen as if he owned it.

I bet I know who owns him. Kirby thought of that rugged, all-too-confident man next door. The one who mentioned the boards down in their mutual fence. A dog owner would be concerned about a damaged fence.

There *was* a resemblance between the man and his canine. The dog sauntered over to the kitchen counter and grabbed the biscuit box off the edge of it. As if he had great practice at doing this very same thing many times before, he upended the box onto the floor and little bone-shaped treats scattered everywhere.

Her little spaniel sat politely eating only one treat, but the bold dog attacked the pile of biscuits as if he'd been starved for days.

"Yep, you belong to Sam Gardner. No doubt about that." Kirby knelt to retrieve what she could of the scattered biscuits. The dog only ate faster, sucking up as many treats as his mouth could hold. "You are a bad dog. I hope you know that."

He didn't seem the slightest bit repentant.

"It's probably not your fault. Look at your owner. You can't help it." She put the box on top of the refrigerator, far out of reach. She patted her little dog and gave her another biscuit for being so polite.

"No more for you, buster." Kirby told the intruder. "C'mon, we're taking you back where you belong."

The dog looked appalled as she snapped a bright pink leash to his chain collar, but he went with her willingly. He was a very good-natured dog. The spaniel followed them to the door, whining when it was clear she had to stay behind.

"Sorry, Jessie." When Sam's dog lunged off the front steps, dragging her with him,

Kirby thought he must have been an obedience-school dropout.

"Just like your owner, aren't you?" She coiled the leash when she caught up with him, holding him firmly. "You are good-looking. I bet all the girls tell you that."

As if in complete agreement, the dog hauled her around the hedge, obviously too self-confident for his own good.

Just like his owner.

The phone was ringing loud and clear through the window he'd left open to air out the kitchen. Sam dumped the end of the garden hose and crashed through the old screen door. He caught the receiver on the fourth ring. "Yeah?"

"Oh, I was about ready to hang up." Aunt Ruth's chipper voice singsonged in his ear. "I thought maybe you gave me a number that wasn't hooked up yet. But I should have known the go-getter you are would have your telephone in already."

"It was tough work to dial the phone company. Nearly took all my energy. Now I'm too weak to fix the plumbing."

A warm chuckle rang on the other end of

the line. "Oh, you can always make me laugh, boy."

"A man does what he can." Warmth seeped into the center of his chest. He loved his aunt, who'd been a second mother to him and had written him faithfully every week when he'd been in the military. And during the tough times afterward.

"I suppose you've already got your tool belt on and working."

"The tools are on the floor, but I am tinkering away."

If he could call it tinkering. It was more like a major repair. He took one look at the trashed sink, broken faucet, the holes in the wall, the door ripped off the front of a filthy fridge. And that was just the beginning.

The question was, how much did he tell her? Aunt Ruth had become more frail after his uncle's death. "The repairs are well under way."

"There's no grass growing under your feet, Sam Gardner. No, I can always count on you." She sounded so proud of him. "I admire a hardworking man. You are something special."

"Nope, just bored." He blushed because her affection embarrassed him. Because he didn't feel special at all. He had a lot of hard lessons and proof to the contrary. "The truth is, I agreed to move here and help you out so I had something to do. Flying around the world was getting too dull. Been there, done that."

"I learned long ago not to believe you, Samuel James Gardner. Beneath that crusty manner of yours is a soft heart gooier than melted chocolate. Which reminds me, thanks for running to the grocery store for me. I found the surprise you bought along with the groceries. You are a dear, precious boy."

That settled it. The woman was just too darn gushy. Sam grabbed a Phillips screwdriver from one of his tool bags and opened a sagging cabinet door. What he'd do is fix that bent screw. "Found the bag of Snickers bars, did you? I was trying to bribe you. I want you to like me better than my other cousins."

"No problem there, as long as you keep bringing me my favorite candy. You are my favorite, boy. Always have been and always will be."

"You are my favorite, too." That was about as affectionate as he could stand being. He loved his aunt, but love was tenuous. And he'd believed in love—his mother's, his wife's—

and seen how easy it was for love to crumble away into hatred.

The bent screw gave and the broken cabinet door handle tumbled into his hand.

"Sounds like you're hard at work." Now the worry was there in Ruth's voice. "The damage to the house isn't too bad, is it?"

"Not too bad," he said, because it was only the truth.

The damage wasn't too bad at all. It was more than bad. It was appalling. The place was trashed. But it wouldn't be by the time Ruth saw it. He'd fix everything damaged between the roof and the foundation first.

"Oh, I'm so relieved. The Realtor was simply exaggerating about the damages, then. I don't know what I would do if I had to find the money to repair that house. It was fine enough to inherit a rental property, but it's been nothing but trouble. Sam, you're my saving grace in all this. I can't tell you what it means to have you take care of this for me."

"For you? You're the one letting me buy this place. The real estate market around here is pretty tight."

"Yes, but heaven knows the house has to be in good repair. And clean. I could hire my cleaning woman to come over. She's quick as a whip and thorough, too."

The place in Sam's chest where a whole heart used to be felt constricted. His aunt was a good person, and there weren't too many of those in this world. "Let's hold off on a cleaning lady for a while, okay?" A *long* while. "I'd like to do a few more repairs and then paint the whole place."

"Oh, of course. Maybe I'd best buy the paint. You go down to the hardware store and put it on my account."

Although it was generous of Ruth, Sam figured that by the time he was done, he would have charged up an easy ten grand. "Why don't you let me worry about that? I thought that was our agreement. I fix this up for sweat equity, right? I've got it under control."

"Such a relief, such a dear boy. Say, have you met little Kirby McKaslin next door?"

The memory of his beautiful neighbor flashed through him like sunlight. She was as graceful, as soft and as perfect as the warm spring day. "Yep. I did happen to meet her. I had to go next door and borrow her hose."

"She's a cute girl, don't you think? And as good as gold. Comes from a fine family—"

He knew where this was going. "Don't even start."

"Start what? I'm just telling you about your new neighbor. I want you to be friendly to her, since she's a friend of the family."

"Friendly? Is that all? I heard a scheme in your voice."

"You heard no such thing."

"Call it instinct, then."

"Instinct? Why, that's preposterous. I wouldn't try to fix you up with a nice, pretty young woman—"

"Fix me up, huh?" At least he'd got her to admit it. Sharp, fire-hot pain scorched a sharp point through the center of him, all the way down to his soul. He knew she had no clue what she was doing to him. "I've asked you not to fix me up."

Ruth's sigh came across the line, not as a whisper of surrender but rather as a gathering of determination. "I know how you feel about women. You're wrong, and you're smart enough to figure that out one day. There are plenty of wonderful, kindhearted women in this world looking for a strong and decent man like you to love and cherish."

His chest compressed. His lungs deflated. The pain left his eyes burning.

To love and cherish? No, he'd tried that once and he wouldn't go there again. He refused to remember another "nice" girl, the one he'd vowed to honor and love for the rest of his life. "Ruth, you're killin' me here."

"Don't you think it's time you moved on?"

"I have." His throat seized up. If he didn't stop his aunt from going down this path, he'd wind up one big, raw wound, open and bleeding. "I know you mean well, but you've got to stop this. I can't take it."

"A big strong warrior like you?"

"I'm not a warrior anymore." The sadness of that battered him, too.

"You're a fine man, and I'm proud to call you my nephew." Love shone in her words.

But it wasn't strong enough to diminish his hopelessness. Or change his mind.

Ruth, protected and gentle hearted, didn't know what he knew. He'd seen too much as a man, as a soldier, as a husband to believe there was any goodness at all in the world. Any goodness that lasted.

He reassured his aunt about the house so she wouldn't worry, and ended the call before she could get another word in edgewise about Kirby McKaslin.

How did Ruth think that he'd just be able to trust anyone enough to love again? And why Kirby McKaslin? Her pretty face flickered back into his thoughts like a movie reel stuck on one vibrant, flawless frame, refusing to fade.

Why was he thinking about her? Picturing her in his mind as if he was interested? He wasn't. A smart man would put all thoughts of her aside and keep his distance from her. Forever.

There was nothing else he could do. He had no heart left.

Since he was a smart man, he didn't look out the window over the sink, which gave him a view of the side of her house. He blocked all images of her as he dropped the screwdriver into his tool belt and ambled out the door and into the welcome sunshine.

He'd finish replacing the valves in the basement, coil up the hose and return it.

Kirby McKaslin was nice enough. She was his neighbor. He'd have to see her time and again. The casual kind of run-ins that neighbors wound up having. He'd be nice to her, friendly, polite, neighborly.

But that was all.

With his game plan ready, Sam stretched the kinks out of his back. Where was his dog?

"Oh!" A woman's gasp of surprise tore him out of his quick flash of panic.

What was Kirby McKaslin doing in his yard, glowing golden and dainty and heavenly, her hair rumpled and windblown? Then he looked down and realized she had a tight grip on a bright pink leash. The leash was attached to a powerful rottweiler. She bent to free the dog, and Leo bounded forward to run circles around Sam's legs.

"Howdy, boy. What have you done now?" Sam knelt to stroke his hands down the dog's broad back. It was the best choice, since that meant he didn't have to look at Kirby.

It was his rotten luck that he couldn't forget her entirely. Her feet were in his line of vision. Delicate feet to match the rest of her encased in trim leather loafers made of the softest-looking leather he'd ever seen. She was quality all the way—any man could see it.

Remember, be polite and neighborly. That was the plan. He refused to remember another delicate woman. See, with just that tiny thought, pain ripped through him, raw and jagged. A constant reminder of the biggest mistake of his life.

One he'd never make again.

Chapter Three

"Your dog must have found a space in the fence," she said in that velvety-soft voice of hers. "It was no trouble figuring out who he belonged to."

She was trying to make conversation. Whether she was just being polite or trying to start a relationship thing, Sam didn't know. He couldn't let himself care.

He stared hard at his dog. Leo glowed with happiness. He obviously liked Kirby. That was one check mark in her favor, that she was kind to animals, but he wasn't going to let it change his resolve.

He stood slowly, careful of his stiff left leg. "Thanks for bringing him back."

"It was my pleasure. He's a good dog. A little energetic."

"He's got a lot of puppy in him still." Sam kept his focus on his dog's broad head. "Guess I'll be right over to fix that fence. I'm sorry he jumped into your yard. C'mon, Leo, inside. Now."

The dog followed him, happily tossing their pretty neighbor his most charming dog grin.

It was embarrassing, that's what, a tough guard dog with his tongue lolling like that. That kind of affection would lead a guy to heartache. Didn't the dog know that?

"Leo? That's his name?"

That was Kirby's voice, dulcet with amusement, calling him back, making his shoes pivot so that he turned toward her, as if he had no say in it. As if his feet were in charge.

"What's wrong with the name Leo?"

"Nothing, exactly."

Leo danced at the tinkling warmth of Kirby's laughter. Sam had to admit he liked the sound of it, too. Soft, not grating. Gentle, not earsplitting.

"It wasn't what I expected from a big dangerous-looking dog like that." She held out one hand and Leo dashed straight for her, gazing adoringly at her while she scratched his chin. "Is he purebred?"

She was captivating. He couldn't seem to

figure out a way to answer. He was a big tough guy. He knew how to speak. What was wrong with him?

You're in trouble, man. His game plan was going to be blown to bits if he didn't thank her and exit stage left. All he had to do was haul Leo through that door, close it and he'd be safe. Unattached. Distant.

But did he do that? No. Did he summon up his best drill-sergeant impressions and sound harsh and mean so that she'd never look at him again with those sparkling eyes full of hope? It's what he *should* have done.

But did he? No. He wanted to hear her laugh again. Against every instinct he had, he advanced when he should have retreated. "So what would you have named him? Wait, I know. Something fancy. Like Prince or Duke, maybe."

"Now *you're* mocking me." She thrust her gently rounded chin just high enough for the wind to sneak beneath the fall of her silken hair and ruffle it.

The wispy locks caressed the side of her face and made him wonder if her hair was as soft as it looked.

"No, I like people names for dogs," she added. "They have feelings, too."

"Let me guess. You've got one of those pampered little dogs. With carefully brushed hair tied up with a pink ribbon. I'm right, aren't I?"

"I'm not telling you."

"A cocker spaniel, right?" He'd recognized the note and type of bark earlier, when she'd been unlocking her front door.

"How did you know?"

"I just do. I'm gifted." Oh, that made her laugh. "What? You don't think so?"

"Gifted isn't the word I'd use. Irritating. Annoying. Arrogant."

"Ouch. Calling me names already? That doesn't bode well for our future together as next-door neighbors." He liked the way a little wrinkle furrowed between her brows right at the bridge of her nose. "You're mad because I'm right."

"I'm not mad, and there's nothing wrong with having a polite dog."

"My dog doesn't have to be well mannered. Not with his good looks. He's naturally adored no matter what."

Was Sam Gardner talking about himself, too? "Yes, but good looks can only take a guy so far."

"That's a matter of opinion." He braced his

hands on his hips, a fighting stance, broadening his shoulders, drawing tight his chest muscles.

He looked as invincible as steel, but there was a tenderness in him, a kindness that shone in the chocolate warmth of his eyes, that gleamed like a promise in his deep rumbling voice. "My dog is good-looking *and* at the top of the food chain. Look at him. Big teeth. Bred for fighting. He's a trained guard dog."

"He's a thief. He helped himself to most of the dog biscuits."

"I can get you another box. Hold on."

"I don't want you to reimburse me with dog treats. I was just—" Okay, so Sam Gardner did meet another criterion. He could make her laugh.

But that didn't mean he was a good man. For example, he might not be a responsible pet owner. "Didn't you notice Leo was gone from your yard?"

"One minute I looked out the window and he was fine. But the phone rang and he must have escaped while I was talking to my lady love."

"You were talking with your aunt, huh?"

"How did you know that?"

"I'm gifted—what can I say?"

"You overheard me through the open windows when you were bringing Leo back."

"And you heard my dog's little bark."

Sam chuckled, low and deep, studying her with a gaze so intent, it was as if he could see her soul, and she shivered, feeling exposed. Way too exposed.

She took a step back, confused, not at all sure she liked this man. He definitely wasn't anything close to her ideal of Mr. Right.

What she knew for sure was that it was time to leave. "Goodbye, Leo. It was nice meeting you. Come over any time to visit."

"I'll be fixing that fence. It's next on my list," Sam informed her as she held out her hands and the big dog laid his face in her open palms.

"I'm glad. This is a quiet neighborhood, but there's always a car now and then that's driving too fast and isn't watching for kids or pets." She knelt, her hair falling all around her face and her shoulders and tumbling down over her nape, to let Leo kiss her chin. "Good dog, good boy."

Sam's heart stopped beating. He'd never seen such gentle hands. Slender and fine boned, with long tapered fingers. She looked like kindness personified, and it rocked him to the core—as if he'd taken a direct blow from a grenade launcher.

Leo gazed at her again with adoration, and while Sam wasn't about to do the same, he could see there *was* something endearing about her. With her head bent forward, he could see the careful part of her hair—perfect, not a strand out of place.

See? She was just what he thought. The perfect woman with a perfect life looking for the perfect man to marry.

He wanted nothing to do with that.

To make it clear, Sam stuffed his hands into his jeans pockets. He kept them there as Kirby rose like a flower to the sun, straight and elegant and lovely, and smiled at him. Hers was a smile that could melt the polar ice caps with its loveliness. Then she moved away and out of his sight.

The scent of her perfume, something light and floral and sweet, remained.

He was alone. And that was good. His life was fine the way it was.

Leo nudged his knee.

"C'mon, boy, let's go grab some lunch. Then we've got to get busy. We've a lot of work ahead of us."

The dog loped up the back steps, dashed across the porch and into the house. He bounded and hopped impatiently while Sam grabbed his wallet and his keys.

The empty house echoed around him, lonely.

As his life was meant to be.

"Ouch!" Kirby sucked her fingernail, a casualty of trying to open the new box of tea. The wrapping remained untouched, despite her torn and bent nail.

What did they make this stuff out of? Invisible steel? Forget breaking another fingernail over this. She was going for the big guns.

She yanked open the top kitchen drawer and rummaged around in the mess. Where had the scissors gone? The ringing phone interrupted her search.

"Hello, Kirby dear. I just wanted to give you a quick call and let you know that my nephew is moving in next door to you."

"Hello, Ruth." Kirby tucked the cordless phone against her shoulder and spotted the scissors in the back of the drawer. "I've already met Sam."

"What did you think?"

Was that excitement in Ruth's voice? "I

think he's, uh, well, it was interesting to meet him."

"Oh, my." The excitement faded into distress. "He wasn't rude to you, was he? He comes across rather rough sometimes. He's had a hard life, the poor man."

She knew Ruth was dying to tell her, but Kirby wasn't about to ask. It wasn't her business and she didn't listen to gossip. She didn't want to know Sam's hardships.

That wasn't true. She *was* curious. What was the real scoop on that man?

Instead she said, "Sam told me he's repairing the house for you, too."

"That's right—he's a real hard worker. He'll do a fine job. I know the kind of first impression he gives, but I promise you he'll make a fine neighbor. My Sam's dependable, strong, hardworking and honest. Why, he's as good as the day is long, and the stories I could tell about him…"

What stories? Kirby wondered, but it wasn't any of her business. Really. "I'm happy he'll make a quiet and responsible neighbor. How are you feeling today?"

"Fine, now that my nephew has moved to town to help me out."

Kirby jabbed the pointed tip of the scissors

into the shrink-wrap. The plastic stuff gave way. Finally. "I suppose this means I'll be seeing more of you, since you'll be coming to visit Sam."

"Yes. He's a great cook. Did you know that?"

"No." It was sweet, how much Ruth loved her nephew. "You're proud of him, I can tell. It must mean the world to have him living close."

"I'll say! He's been away, traveling the globe since he graduated from high school, but we've kept in touch over the years. I wrote him faithfully every week. And now here he is, taking care of so many troubles for me."

Sam did look as though he could solve any problem. After she hung up, Kirby rose on her tiptoes and could see him perfectly through her kitchen window. He was in his backyard tossing a huge orange plastic bone. His enormous black dog leaped like a puppy, knocking into shrubs and bounding over flowers as he raced after his toy. Leo loped back with the bone lodged in his powerful jaws and dropped it onto Sam's waiting hand.

It wasn't the dog she noticed, but the man. How he rubbed his dog's head with a strong but kind touch. Sam looked different. With his guard down, he almost appeared good-hearted. As strong as steel, as powerful as a midnight storm, but benevolent.

He's dependable, strong, hardworking and honest. Those were a few more of her requirements, right there. Kirby wanted a husband she could respect and look up to. Not that Sam Gardner was that man.

What else had Ruth said about him? *He's had a hard life.*

What happened to him? Kirby wondered.

"This is the last one." His distant rumble rose on the breeze blowing through the open window. "One more throw, then we've got to fix the fence. Can't have you running loose, you big menace. It's bad manners to accost pretty ladies."

The menace barked in happy agreement, hopping and leaping in anticipation, his attention on the enormous plastic bone. Sam's laughter and the warm vibration of his voice lifted and fell according to the wind's whim. There was something vulnerable in him, this big strong man, playing with his dog.

A hard life, huh? She wondered about that as she watched him kneel to rub Leo's ruff. Then he disappeared into the house, the dog shadowing him.

When Sam appeared again, he was wearing his tool belt and hauling a small bucket that rattled when he came around to her side gate.

"Hey, I'm about to trespass," he called from below the window.

She was out of his line of sight, and he hadn't looked over at her once. How did he know where she was? Did he know she'd been watching him?

"I'm surprised you're using the gate. I thought you might just climb over the fence instead."

"I would, but I don't want to set a bad example for Leo. Hey, hello there, pup."

Her spaniel's bark rose in a happy greeting as Kirby hit the switch on the iced tea maker.

"That's some watchdog you got there," he called through the screen door. "What does she do? *Invite* burglars into the yard?"

"Only once, and he wasn't a burglar." Kirby stared at him hard.

"Hey, insult me and I won't fix the fence."

"My dog isn't the one getting out." She pushed open the screen door to join him on the back deck. "I almost have your tea ready. It's brewing right now."

"Brewing? You don't use the mix?"

"From a can? Don't insult me. When I promised you tea, I meant the real thing." She led the way to the back of the property, where a few boards leaned against the fence beneath the shade of a giant maple.

"The real thing? I don't know." He hefted the awkward boards as if they weighed nothing at all. "I think that's too wholesome for me. I need the fake stuff with all the chemicals and artificial flavors, or I could go into shock. Then who'd fix your fence?"

"I'm a nurse practitioner. I'd save your life."

"Great. You'd revive me so I could go back to work."

"I'd revive you because I took an oath. And because you're my new *quiet* neighbor. The one who *won't* play loud music at night."

"Are you hinting at something?" Acting as if puzzled, he hauled the hammer from his battered leather tool belt. "I'll have to remind my fellow biker gang members to keep it down when we gather at midnight to shoot off our illegal firearms."

Oh, he thought he was funny when he was no such thing. The tea was probably ready, so she headed back to the house. "Can I get you anything? I have cookies."

"Cookies are too sweet for me. They might ruin my sour disposition."

"How about a lemon?"

The little spaniel skipped after her, clearly in love with her owner and, to Sam's shock, Leo took after Kirby, too, his tongue lolling, his gait snappy, that sappy loving look in his big eyes.

"Hey, get back here!" he commanded, and the dog gave him a sad expression. It was an embarrassment, that's what. "Oh, don't complain. Come here."

He didn't see what all the fuss was about. Kirby was nice and seemed lovely, but she was a woman. Like half the people on the planet.

He shoved a bunch of climbing rose canes aside. Yep, she was a woman. Flowers and tidy weeded flower beds and those little figurine things stuck here and there. A birdbath and stepping stones with designs on them.

He was glad he was in charge of his own destiny. Being alone was a good thing. He didn't need anyone and he didn't need ceramic stepping stones.

As he dug through his bucket for the right

size of galvanized nails, he heard her phone ring inside the house. He could see her kitchen through the big back window. Tidy and cozy and as ruffly and bright as a magazine cover.

It looked homey. There she was, leaning against the white counter, the phone tucked against her shoulder, talking while she poured sparkling tea into a tall glass.

She sure made a pretty picture. His chest ached with the power of it. He supposed it was the image she made, standing there like an advertisement for all that was good in the world. Clean counters and polished wood and every knickknack in place. With a smile that shone as genuine as the sun.

Not that he believed in that kind of goodness anymore.

Goodness? No. Peace? Yes. That's what he believed in.

After too many years as a soldier and then as a corporate pilot flying head honchos anywhere in the world they needed to go, he just wanted a home. Peace and quiet. To be content and enjoy his life. Just him and Leo.

He drove the nail in sure and deep with one whack of the hammer. Pinned his elbow on the board and drove in a second nail. A third.

"That was my sister." She came up from behind him, her steps hushed in the soft grass. Ice cubes rattled as she set down glass and pitcher, both topped with sliced lemons.

Thoughtful.

"I've got to run in and help her with the coffee shop. She's shorthanded. Do you need anything else? I'll leave the back door unlocked. Just help yourself."

"Sure, okay." He didn't look at her as he drove another nail home. "I'll lock up when I finish."

"Okay. Thanks, Sam."

"I've got to ask you something." He nailed the next board into place. "This has really been bothering me. I've had some neighbor disasters, too."

"You're worried about *me?*"

"Are you a partying kind of girl? I'm praying that you're a quiet sort of woman who doesn't play music all hours of the night. I need my beauty sleep."

"Funny." She slung her slim black purse over her shoulder. "Give my regards to your biker friends."

Her wink made him chuckle, and it warmed

him down to his bones. One thing about Kirby—he liked her sense of humor.

But that was all.

She swept away from him, like grace and spring and peace all rolled up into one perfect human being. He wasn't looking for a wife. Not by a long shot. But she was fine.

Very fine, indeed.

———

Chapter Four

Her house was dark—not surprising considering the late hour. The green glow from the clock on the stove, showing 3:15, cast enough illumination to guide her around the corner of the island. She padded on bare feet to the cupboard and reached for her favorite oversize mug by feel.

As she flicked on the cold water faucet, she swore she could smell the faint hint of Sam's woodsy scent, and it was pleasant. The image of him working on her backyard fence shot into her mind. The afternoon sun had burnished his broad back and his arm muscles had flexed while he drove the nails home.

Fixing her fence for a glass of iced tea. What kind of man did that?

A man who named his ferocious-looking

dog Leo, that's who. A man whose aunt sang his praises as if he were perfect in every way.

You've thought about him enough today, okay? Kirby popped open the microwave door, and the interior light burned like a beacon in the darkness as she placed the cup inside. She loved the embossed image of a wet, rumpled cartoon cat in a puddle that said Nothing Is Ever Simple.

That was her life slogan. She shut the door, hit the two-minute button and listened to the machine whir. Sam. There she was, thinking about him again. And what was wrong with that? Everything.

Especially having a conversation about him with herself at three in the morning.

The light from the microwave showed her tidy sink and counter. After coming home from helping out at the coffee shop and having dinner with her sisters, she'd expected to find Sam's glass and tray left on the counter. But no, he'd rinsed the dishes, put them in the dishwasher. All by himself.

Okay, that was a bonus requirement. One that wasn't on her list. Maybe she should add it. Right under hardworking and kind she would add "does dishes." Not a bad attribute for her future Mr. Right to have.

And as if that wasn't enough, the fence repair was perfect. Through the night shadows around her back porch light she could just make out the unbroken row of boards that proved Sam Gardner completed even small jobs with care.

All those jokes he'd made about being a biker or in a rock band made her smile, even in the lonely night. He was probably a pretty good plumber. And he was here to stay.

She could see his house perfectly through the spreading branches of the lilac trees outside her kitchen window. His windows were dark, his house silent.

Pure blessed quiet.

She appreciated the stillness, but of course tonight had to be the night she couldn't sleep. She hated insomnia. Too much on her mind— the practical worries of life like mortgage payments and school loan payments and remembering she needed to give notice at the hospital where she did shift work.

She told herself it was better to worry about all of her responsibilities than what was truly troubling her.

She wouldn't think about the accident.

Or about the dreams that had troubled her more frequently after the medevac crash last month.

The microwave binged, and Kirby retrieved the steaming cup. She dug a bag of her favorite sweet chamomile tea from the third drawer next to the stove. The paper around the bag crinkled in the quiet, and down the hall came the muffled sound of the little dog yipping in her sleep. Maybe Jessie was chasing birds in the backyard in her little doggy dreams.

The phone rang, loud and harsh in the peaceful kitchen. The tea bag tumbled from her fingers. Startled, she sprinted across the short distance to the other end of the kitchen. The caller ID told her that it was business.

Being on call was a nurse's life.

She snatched up the receiver before the phone could ring a third time.

Stars were everywhere, sending out enough glow to light them up like a beacon, but the rendezvous was a go. Sam never backed down from a mission. It was a challenge, that was all. He was one of the best pilots he knew, and tonight he had to be at his best. He flew so low the whack of treetops against their belly made his navigator nervous.

Flying nap of the earth kept him sharp. On his toes. The intel had been good. Good enough, at least, to keep him several clicks south of trouble. He liked to stay away from enemy soldiers who might happen to be armed with missile launchers. Launched missiles weren't so good for his helicopter.

It looked like easy flying tonight, and his navigator said so. Mark. They'd gone through boot camp together. Buddies to the end.

"You're as crazy as ever, Gardner, but tonight looks like a cakewalk. Wait—"

Then the sky lit up. Fire and a deafening crack of metal exploding—

Sam jerked awake, disoriented, the dream still rolling in his mind, frame after frame of fire and death and fighting for calm.

He wasn't falling out of the sky in hostile territory. He was safe in his new bed in his new room. Even the sheets were new. The memories faded, but the experience of it didn't. No, that fateful night and its far-reaching effects stayed with him. Still.

He swiped his hand over his face and encountered damp. He had sweat bullets and his hair was drenched. It was the move—any change brought up the dreams—but it was more than that. Much more.

A dog snore broke the silence, followed by the scrape, scrape of dog paws on the floor. Leo was dreaming again, digging and running. Sam knew how fine it was to have good dreams, so he was careful not to wake his dog as he felt his way out of the room and into the kitchen.

He still went over the what ifs in his mind. There had been no warning, nothing. Mechanical failures happened. It was a fact. He believed that all things happened for a reason.

It seemed odd that he'd learned that night and for too many nights following how cruel people could be. Even his own wife.

Old wounds. Deep scars. He fought to clear his mind of the nightmare. He checked the refrigerator—nothing in it because he'd drunk the last root beer after grabbing dinner at the local drive-in.

Empty-handed, he kicked open the back door and sat on the top porch step, head in his hands, his heart in pieces. The memory had sunk deep claws into him. He was still hooked, still haunted, unable to keep his mind in the present.

He could hear the beat of the blades as he fought the controls. He'd taken a hit and the radio was suddenly full of chatter, a mission gone wrong, injured SEALs at the LZ, under fire and in need. He was their only ticket to safety and he was going down....

Why was this haunting him tonight?

He let the temperate night air cool the sweat on his brow, and he knew why—the reason lived right next door.

She'd made him think of Carla, of his mistakes, of wrongs that could never be righted. Failings that could only be forgiven.

He saw goodness in Kirby.

When he didn't believe in real goodness. Not anymore.

The phone rang, a sharp blast of sound that saved him. He hauled his tired carcass up off the step and snared the receiver on the third ring. It was someone in need. A sick child needing a lifesaving flight to the hospital in Seattle, the nearest medical facility with the emergency care she required.

He was the pilot who'd volunteered to fly anyone who needed it.

He slammed down the phone, renewed, energized. With a purpose.

A mission was exactly what he needed. To focus his thoughts and give him a sense of purpose. Sam grabbed his keys, his shoes and his jeans and was out the door in ten seconds flat.

The local private airport was dark and still in the early-morning hours as Kirby pulled off the two-lane road and into the paved parking lot.

She hated to fly, but there was no time to waste. She hauled her medical bag out of the trunk. Who was going to pilot the flight? Chet always piloted the flights she volunteered for, but he'd up and sold the airfield two weeks ago. Retired to Lake Havasu, Arizona, where there were no cold winters to trouble his worsening arthritis.

She hadn't heard who'd replaced him as a volunteer. Would it be the new owner of the airport? There were a few chopper pilots around. Maybe it would be Ed, who flew with the county search and rescue.

Her sneakers crunched on the gravel. The airfield was still this time of night. Everything was dark. The modest tower, the hangars lined in tiny rows off to the side, the mown fields that smelled of sweet bunchgrass and wildflowers. A wild rabbit scampered out of her way as she followed the path toward a helicopter set out in the middle of the tarmac.

Not a chopper she recognized. Newer than many she'd flown in. Whoever was flying tonight, he couldn't be too bad of a person. To donate a flight and all that went with it spoke of deep pockets and a generous spirit.

Wait. Was that him? She caught a brief movement. A man's tall form, all but shadow, circled out from behind the chopper, a clipboard in hand. Doing his preflight check. Kirby knew she couldn't be heard over the beat of the blades and the whine of the engines, so she tried to catch his attention with a wave.

He lifted his clipboard in recognition, a dark stranger of a man who remained faceless and formless in the shadows.

Since he'd seen her, she ducked, climbed aboard and settled in. She'd done this probably a hundred times. Chet's medical equipment was up against the bulkhead. He'd probably donated it, knowing him, and she made sure the defibrillator and monitors were in working order.

She was belting into the jump seat in back when the pilot's words, muffled by the noise of the helicopter, told her he was ready to go. Before Kirby could wonder if the pilot was going to introduce himself or if she should go up front, another man's shadow appeared.

"Hey, Kirby." Jeremiah Clark, anesthesiologist, slammed the hatch behind him. "Looks like we've got a great new pilot. I have a lot of confidence in him. Have you met him?"

"No, I haven't had the chance to."

"He has a lot of combat flying experience. I always feel better with a veteran at the controls." Once a marine, the doc dropped his gear and eased onto the seat next to her. "I'm glad Chet left us with a good replacement. Sam seems like a great guy. Once we're airborne, you oughta go up and—"

"Sam?"

"Yep. Sam Gardner. He's Ruth Gardner's nephew. Ruth and my mom are in the gardening club together…."

Sam Gardner is the new pilot? The blood rushed from her head, leaving her dazed. She felt the faint movements and sounds of him up front, out of sight behind the panel of metal.

Sam, a pilot? She tried to picture it. She could. Sam's confidence, the competence.

But he's a plumber. Isn't that what he'd said?

"He doesn't own the airfield, too, does he?"

Jeremiah nodded. "Of course he does. Didn't you hear?"

No, she hadn't heard anything. That's why she'd assumed he was a plumber. Not a pilot and a businessman with deep pockets and his own helicopter.

"Hope you're strapped in, par'ners." Sam's voice boomed in her earpiece. "Let's get this bird in the air."

It was him. No doubt about it. Kirby couldn't believe it.

But it did seem to fit. He was larger than life. Why not be a local Good Samaritan?

"Good having you at the controls, Sam," Jeremiah said into his mouthpiece. "I don't like flying, so take it easy on me, man."

"I'll do my best, Doc. Hold on tight, Kirby. We're good to go." Sam sounded confident, unshakable as the chopper's blades whipped harder. "NASA, we have liftoff."

They rose in a swinging bump that felt as if the earth had fallen out beneath them and they were rising straight up in a breathless sweep.

Jeremiah covered the mouthpiece. "We'll miss Chet, but Sam's good."

She was better off not thinking about Sam right now. She was thinking about staying alive. Once she had a patient to care for, she'd be all right. But until then, she had entirely too much time on her hands to imagine the engine exploding. A blade breaking. Pieces of steel peeling off the side of the helicopter.

See? It was better when she didn't think. When she didn't remember the worst day of her life. A day when she'd been laughing with her sister one minute, thrilled with the trip they were taking, and then everything had gone wrong.

"Thank you for flying Gardner Airlines," Sam's voice quipped in her ear. "Please make sure you return your tray and seat back to the upright position. I regret to inform you that we have no in-flight movie tonight, but I can sing for you. How about an innovative rendition of 'Moon River'?"

"Pay attention to the flying, Sam," she told him. "Don't serenade me."

"I can sing and fly at the same time. Wanna see?"

"No." She could imagine him strapped in his seat, with that in-charge look he had and that lopsided grin, the one that made his rugged face crack a little to show the kindness beneath. "Just fly the helicopter."

"Too bad. I sing a hair-raising 'Moon River.'" He feigned disappointment as the chopper banked to the right, slicing through the night sky. "Take a look out your portside window. That's some view."

A sickle moon was playing hide-and-seek behind a veil of trailing clouds, glowing silver in the black velvet sky. The impressive shapes of the constellations dominated the view from her window as the chopper charged through the dark. The night surrounding her was endless.

As infinite as the universe.

So high above the earth, Kirby felt as if anything were within their reach.

Surely Sam would keep them safe as they journeyed through the night and stars to the sick child who needed them.

He should have known. The peaches-and-cream girl next door was selfless, too.

Sam couldn't get Kirby McKaslin out of his mind, even with the demands of the flight. As they headed toward the horizon with their little passenger on board, dawn tailed them. Subtle at first, just the softest glow of peach light until the sky was ablaze around them, a golden fire that warmed the shadows from the control panels and the chill from his heart.

That's what hope felt like. He was glad to see the blue sky of day. Probably because he'd flown so many missions at night with danger anywhere. He felt safer, reassured, with the good old U.S.A. beneath him. The Rocky Mountains were behind him, the Cascade Range up ahead, and after an easy landing at the hospital, the little girl would get the help she needed. Mission complete.

He felt hopeful for the first time in two years. Hopeful he might finally find the peace he'd been praying for.

The child they'd picked up north of Townsend looked pretty sick to him. Her mother was in the back, a sad-faced woman with permanent worry lines grooved into her brow and around her mouth. Kirby had known both mother and daughter by name from the free clinic, she'd said, and greeted them with sincerity. She'd leaped out of the back to help board the child, so tender and careful.

Sam had hoped Kirby might get the chance to come up front and chat with him, if the situation warranted it and the child's condition stabilized. But as the smudge of light and concrete and steel of Seattle appeared on the horizon, he figured that the opportunity had passed by. She was probably busy caring for the child and the mother's emotional needs, too.

Maybe it was for the best.

He landed the bird, killed the engine and watched, his duty done, as medical staff appeared. They pushed an empty gurney as they came, faces grim. They wasted no time in loading the child. He wanted to help, but was wise enough to know he'd only get in the way.

He let the men and women trained to help the child do their jobs, and Kirby went with them, holding the little girl's pale hand in hers as she ran beside the gurney. Her touch compassionate, her gentle heart visible.

It almost made a believer of him. *Almost.*

The cynic in him refused to believe what his eyes saw. She looked good, but nobody was *that* good.

He thought of Kirby long after she'd disappeared from his sight. He waited, alone, as the morning lengthened and the sun shone rare and bright for Seattle in springtime.

She'd been the only vision of any kindness he'd seen in a very long time.

* * *

Kirby was surprised to see Sam Gardner reclining in the busy waiting area, a big strong hulk of a man dressed in an old T-shirt with the faded logo of the United States Army across the front of it, topped by a black leather jacket.

He'd stretched his long, jean-encased legs out in front of him, crossed at the heels, his leather work boots unlaced, on the same floor where, a few feet away, several small children ran and shrieked and crawled around him. It didn't appear to bother him in the least.

He spotted her a moment later, and the tension snapped back into him. His shoulders rose, his ankles uncrossed, his jaw clenched. His posture went from slack to soldier straight in two seconds flat. He looked every inch the capable pilot who had seen them safely there and saved a little girl's life.

"How's Sarah doing?"

"She's stable."

"Poor kid." True sadness etched its way into the rugged lines of his face. "Is she gonna make it?"

"The prognosis is good, although she's pretty sick." Kirby ached for the little girl with leukemia who'd been her patient too many times at their hometown hospital. A medical facility, as good as it was, that didn't have the specialists or equipment the big-city hospitals had. "We've brought her in before, and we probably will again."

"I'll keep the chariot's tank full for her, in case she needs it."

What a generous man. Donating his time, his helicopter and a lot of fuel, which was expensive, for a child who had no insurance. Sarah's parents could not afford the regular medevac flights. "You're a good man, Sam Gardner."

"Yeah, but don't tell anyone that. It'll ruin my hard-earned reputation."

He teased when the situation was serious. He turned away, as if to hide deeper emotions.

Caring was one of her requirements. So was generous.

Sam Gardner was more than he seemed. Much more.

She dug through her pockets and then her bag and unburied her cell phone. She checked it. No messages.

"Waiting for a call from your boyfriend?"

Why was he asking about a boyfriend? Was he interested? Kirby zipped the small phone into her coat pocket. "No boyfriend. I've been trying to find a place for Sarah's mother to stay. There's a Ronald McDonald House down the street, and I think there's a chance she can stay there for a few nights."

"I should have figured you'd do something like that."

"Why do you say it like that, as if it's a bad thing?"

"No, I didn't mean it that way. I meant, what don't you do? You charm dogs and help your neighbors and volunteer for your community. Oh, and you offer medical care free to sick children and look after their families. Yep, that's a bad thing. Shocking. You're not a good example for me."

"Me? What about you? You gave a needy family a free medical flight."

"It's just community service. It keeps my parole officer happy."

"You don't have a parole officer. Stop trying to act as if you aren't a good guy. I've got you figured out, Sam Gardner."

"You do? Foiled again." He jammed his fists into his jacket pockets.

A good guy? No. He was a great man. And the list of his attributes was growing. The man next door was becoming a hero in her eyes.

Hero wasn't on her list, but it would make a good quality in a husband.

Sam jabbed the elevator call button. "Where's the doc?"

"Jeremiah's going to stay with Sarah for a while. He'll give me a call if there's a change in her condition."

"Do we wait for him or head back?"

"Jeremiah's fiancée is on staff here. He's going to stay with her for a few days, then head back on his own."

"I guess that leaves you and me, kid." He winked, imitating Bogie with perfection.

"Hey, that's pretty good."

"I am."

Incorrigible, but he was starting to grow on her. And that was saying something. Most men never made it so high on her list. "What are you doing flying? I thought you said you were a plumber?"

"No, I said I was fixing the plumbing on my house. Two different things. You just *assumed*. Assumptions can get you into trouble."

"You're enjoying this, aren't you?"

"Yep. You can't judge a person by how he looks. And right now I hope I look hungry, because I want to find some place to eat. Wanna join me?"

The elevator doors opened, and Sam waited while she stepped into the crowded car. Kirby squeezed in, careful not to jostle a mother cradling a new baby in her arms, a pretty little girl with a headband bow that matched her rosebud-printed sleeper.

Kirby melted. Oh, what a lucky woman to have such a precious baby in her life. She ached with longing. What sweet gifts would there be to come in her own life? She'd been patient, but it was hard waiting and wondering.

And then she felt guilty. She already had so much in her life. She had sisters she loved, friends and family around her. A cozy house and a calling as a nurse. She had her health and her life and a wonderful future yet to come.

Unlike Allison. Her oldest sister. The sister she had not been able to save. Days like this, when she was tired, when she'd been face-to-face with life and death, she thought of her sister's blood on her hands. Of how tightly Allison had held her hand before she exhaled her last breath.

Pain ripped her in pieces, right there in the elevator, standing beside perfect strangers and one man she hardly knew. She could see her reflection in the mirrored wall panels. She looked like anyone else. No one would guess at the sorrows she held hidden inside. Her flaws. The places where she kept all her failures and her unworthiness buried. Scars no one else could see.

What about the people surrounding her? What sorrows had they had? And Sam. What about him?

The doors opened, people pushed out into the floor. Sam's hand shot out and stopped Kirby before she could move.

"No," he said above the familiar clatter and din from the institution's cafeteria. "I hate hospitals. Let's go somewhere else to eat."

She nodded as the doors closed and the elevator descended. She could feel his sadness. She wondered who had died. They had that in common, at least. They were alone, and Sam took a step away from her, setting distance between them.

"It's been a while since I transported a passenger I needed to worry about." He tugged a black baseball cap out of his jacket pocket and didn't look at her.

"Why didn't you worry about your last passengers?"

"They were vice presidents and that kind of

thing." Sam shook out his cap before he put it on. "Why worry about someone in good health, who makes a good living? I meant the last time I flew in the military."

"I can't believe our government trusted you with a chopper."

"I was your tax dollars at work."

"I'm speechless. Should I write my congressman?"

"Many folks already have. It's too late. I retired."

The elevator crept to a stop and the doors parted to reveal the busy lobby. Wide windows looked out on the morning.

A beautiful morning.

"How much time do you have?" Sam led the way across the polished tile floors.

"I'm not in a hurry to get back. Why?"

He didn't answer. He held the heavy glass doors for her, and she stepped out into the cool morning sun.

The air was filled with the hum of engines and the sounds of the nearby freeway that buzzed like a saw across the mirrored surface of the lake. She caught glittering snatches of Lake Washington peeking between buildings. Sam took off down the sidewalk. She ran to catch up with him.

"Have you ever been to Seattle before?" she asked, praying he knew where he was going.

"Yep." That was all he said, just a terse answer and nothing else as he hooked a right at the corner and kept walking, straight through crowds of people who parted like the Red Sea as he advanced.

To her surprise, he didn't open a door to one of the many delis and coffee shops lining the sidewalk, but waved to hail a cab.

"Your chariot, my lady. I hope you're ready for an adventure." He leaned close enough for her to breathe in the spicy aftershave he wore. The low intimate dip in his voice made her look at him twice.

Made her hope.

It just went to show that a girl never knew where her path would take her. Or when Mr. Right might walk into her life. Was it Sam? She would have to wait and see.

Chapter Five

The streets of Seattle crept by as they inched through the crowded downtown. Kirby felt small on the street at the base of so many tall buildings reaching for the cloud-strewn sky. Where was he taking her? She was going to enjoy every minute of this adventure.

"This is it." Sam shoved a handful of ones at the driver, climbed out and held the door for her.

The wind was cool and briny from glittering Puget Sound. The sidewalks were busy with commuters hurrying from their parking garages or their bus stops to one of the many skyscrapers that marched through the core of the city. Thousands of windows blazed with the golden light of the new day.

"Hurry, we can make the light." Sam

touched her elbow, guiding her in the direction of the corner where the "don't walk" sign flashed red, and other pedestrians hurried with them in a final dash across the street.

Where were they headed? To one of the little shops with cheerful front windows advertising breakfast fare, or the bigger restaurants with iron tables and chairs set out so patrons could enjoy the water view?

As they passed by coffee shops and cafés and bakeries, the mouthwatering aroma of freshly baked pastries and strong enticing coffee nearly killed her. She was really getting hungry.

"I'm hungry, too," Sam said to her, as if he'd read her thoughts. Or shared them. "The wait will be worth it. I give you my word of honor."

"It better be. I know where you live."

They swept around a corner and saw the ferry terminal hunched on the waterfront. A big white-and-green ferry waited meekly at the pier, car after car rolling onto the street. People spilled down the gangplank, hurrying with their briefcases and packs and cups of coffee. This *wasn't* what she'd expected.

"Two, please." Sam pushed a twenty at the woman behind the glass partition, grabbed his change and both tickets. "Have you ever ridden a ferry?"

"No. But you have," she guessed.

"Yep. I grew up around here."

He was a Seattle boy, huh? She didn't picture him in a city. He had the relaxed confidence men raised in the country had.

"C'mon, this way." He headed up the plank, shouldering through the oncoming pedestrians.

She had no choice but to follow him. The man who brazened through the trickle of straggling shore-bound pedestrians as if they ought to get out of his way. Was he always this bossy? That was not an attribute on her checklist for the perfect husband.

When they were at the top of the walkway and she was out of breath, she leaned against the cold iron rail. "You have this incredibly annoying habit."

"Only one?"

"You act as though you're in charge."

"That's because I *am* in charge." A dimple cut into his cheeks as he jammed both fists into his jacket pockets. "Don't worry. You're in good hands."

Why did her heart turn over like that? His melted-chocolate voice, the steady sincerity in his gaze, the way he towered over her, blocking her view of the sky and the city. He was all she could see. Bigger than life and every one of her girlhood dreams of what a man should be.

And he was here, beside her. What did she do with him? She took a step past him and headed for the main passenger lobby. "In good hands? You're not an insurance agent. I don't think I ought to trust you."

"It's not too late to turn back. The ferry is still at dock." He held the door for her, and his arm brushed her shoulder as she passed. "I notice you're not leaving. Decided I'm a safe risk after all?"

"No. I figure if I wind up missing they'll know who to interrogate first."

"It wouldn't do any good. I'm impervious to pain, thanks to prisoner-of-war school."

"Let me guess. You led a daring escape."

"Naturally. I'm always the boss."

"See? You admitted it." She chose a seat next to the window and collapsed into it.

It felt good to be off her feet. Maybe it was the lack of sleep or the letdown after the adrenaline rush of working to keep Sarah's condition stable and the little girl as comfortable as possible on the flight. She'd never been like this with any man.

She was normally shy, but Sam brought out the real her. "I don't like domineering men."

"Hey, I'm not domineering. I'm not making you do a thing. You could have stayed at the hospital, but you're with me voluntarily." He settled into the seat next to her, too big for the plastic frame, and his steely shoulder bumped into hers and remained, hard and unyielding.

"Voluntarily? You're my ride back home. If I lose you, then I have to hoof it, and it's a long walk back to Montana."

"What? You won't have to walk anywhere. With your good looks, beautiful, you can charm any pilot from here to California."

Had she heard him right? Reeling, Kirby turned to the window, her mind spinning. Had he called her beautiful? No one had ever said that to her.

She was plain. She knew that. But the man meant to love her, the one in her dreams, wouldn't think she was plain.

No. He would think there was something special about her. That's the way true love went, right?

So either Sam Gardner needed a serious eye exam or he was simply being charming or he earned another check mark on her list.

"By the way—" he leaned close so his words were a warm tickle against her ear "—we're going to the best bakery ever."

"How do you know? Have you gone to every bakery in the world?"

His eyes twinkled at her. "Yes."

"Liar."

"You're awfully sassy for such a nice girl. My aunt was all wrong about you."

"Why? Just because I question you doesn't mean I'm a bad person."

"A good person would agree with me."

"You're impossible—has anyone ever told you that?"

"All the time, but I've got you laughing. You don't look as sad as you did in the hospital. You have history with little Sarah, don't you?"

"Sarah's been a patient of mine over the last few years. I'm doing shift work, whenever I can, until my new job starts, and I took care of Sarah in the peds unit. I also volunteer at the free clinic and saw her there, too. She's had a hard time."

"But she has you to take care of her. She

seemed happy to see you. You were a comfort to her."

"I was a friendly face."

Much more than that, Sam thought. He ached—his body, his heart, his soul. Not with a physical pain, but an emotional one. And how was that possible?

How had Kirby gotten past the titanium walls protecting his heart? She was making him feel, and he didn't like it. Life was easier when he accepted what was and didn't try to look for the impossible. For the good.

What was Kirby doing to him? And why was he letting her affect him?

He hopped to his feet. He couldn't sit still. He stretched in the wide aisle, the dozens and dozens of seats and booths empty as the ferry rumbled, ready to set sail.

Outside, the endless blue waters of the sound gleamed—as perfect as a sheet of blue diamonds. Sam saw the amethyst mountains and emerald foothills and the crystal brilliance of the city where he used to live with his wife. When he'd believed he'd find a good life with the woman he loved.

When he'd been captured, all he'd thought about, the only thing that had kept him going, was to see her again. To be with her. To hold

her in his arms and never let go. To finally
have a place where he belonged.

The ferry bumped to a start, jarring him out
of his memories, away from the dark and into
the light of the present. The big bulky ship
chugged as slowly as a tugboat away from the
dock and into the impressive waters. Another
ferry, packed with commuters, passed them
by, ready to dock.

Once they were on their way, the water
stretched ahead of them like paradise.

Paradise wasn't meant for a man like him.
Wasn't that clear to him by now? After all
he'd been through?

"Come on, let's see if we can spot any dolphins." He didn't look at her. He wasn't sure
she was following him.

He led the way through the glass doors and
onto the unprotected deck where the wind
stung like ice, but it was such a wonderful and
free feeling to cling to the railing and watch
the ferry slice through the water.

Sam hung over the railing just enough to
see into the ocean far below. "No dolphins.
Maybe once we're farther out."

"I have this irresistible urge to give you a
little shove."

He chuckled, straightened. His dark eyes

tried to sparkle, but they were shadowed. Troubled. "You're not nearly as nice as you look, Kirby McKaslin. Maybe I have a few irresistible urges of my own."

"I know how to swim." She gripped the rail, knowing full well that he'd never toss her over. Her chin shot up, so he knew she wasn't afraid of him. "I used to be a certified lifeguard. That's how I put myself through college."

"As a lifeguard? Did you teach little kids to swim?"

"Yes, and I loved it. I was teaching those children a valuable skill, one that could save their lives one day."

"I was a lifeguard, too." That amused him, that he and Florence Nightingale had that in common. They were about as different as he figured they could be. "I lifeguarded afternoons and weekends when I was a teenager. It kept me out of trouble and put my energy into something constructive. I worked the beaches just over there."

He gestured to the span of public beach west of the city, which was rapidly gliding past them as the tongues and islands of land surrendered to the powerful Puget Sound.

"It makes you sad to remember that."

Gentle those words. Her hand covered his with a warm, assuring touch.

He could feel the comfort flow from her to him, from her tender heart to his well-defended one. It startled him. Troubled him.

He was a tough guy. He didn't need comfort. He didn't need to turn to a woman who would only let him down in the end.

Then why couldn't he seem to make his hand move away from hers? He was a fully functioning male. He had control of his limbs and digits. He could command his fingers. So why was her hand still on his, satin-soft and delicately boned and consoling?

He watched the distant shores drift past. Was he sad? "Yep. My dad died from pneumonia when I was five. It was rough. We had some very hard times. My mom was on her own, and I was a latchkey kid. I'd come home to our apartment after school, and I didn't like the empty feeling when I got there. So I went out and hung around with a not so good crowd."

She might as well know the truth about him. Know that he'd never been a Boy Scout. He wasn't a good guy who flew volunteer flights out of the goodness of his pristine heart. In too many ways he was still serving his country, doing what he could to make a difference.

That didn't make him altruistic.

No, just the opposite. He was deeply flawed, and when Kirby figured that out, she'd either think she could try to heal him and save him or she'd keep her distance from him.

It was fine. He could handle it. He was prepared. He'd never let her close enough to hurt him.

"You probably have a charmed life, though, so you don't know what it's like to be surrounded by sad memories. That's why I don't live here."

She pulled her hand away and swiped windblown hair out of her eyes. Maybe he was imagining it, but she looked sad, too. Her mouth thinned into a tight, hard line. "Maybe I do know about that. Maybe my life hasn't been charmed."

"I hear you come from a good family with money and one of the best ranches in the county. Ruth waxes on about what fine people the McKaslins are. You were probably cheerleader and homecoming queen."

"No, but my four sisters were."

"Not you?" He said the words kindly, as if he knew what it was like to be lost.

"I've known sadness." She stared hard into the water, as if that would make her confession come more easily. "My oldest sister, Allison, died in a plane accident several years ago. It was a private plane headed for a retreat. It had mechanical trouble and went down."

I was on that plane, too, she meant to say. But the words didn't come.

"I'm truly sorry." He took her hand and held hard, tight, protective.

That single day had been the worst of her life. She had the scars to prove it. Physical and emotional. "Nothing has been the same since. *I'm* not the same."

She blinked hard, staring deep into the water churning and swirling around the boat's iron hull. No one could possibly know the depth of her grief. Or her guilt. Some nights she woke up with a loss too wide to fill.

"Sometimes," she told him, "people aren't what you think."

"No. Sometimes they are a good deal more."

Sam liked her. He really did. Kirby was beautiful, not in a stunning-supermodel way. Not in an every-hair-in-place, makeup-done-just-so kind of way.

No, her beauty was subtle, the way the

dawn came in the far north. So quiet, you had to listen and watch for it. But when it came, the unassuming light glowed like grace over a frozen world. It made a man's heart fill and brim over.

And she didn't seem to know that's what she was. That's what she did to him.

She swept stray locks of hair out of her eyes with a slender hand. He remembered the gentleness she'd shown to little Sarah. Kirby's sensitive healing hands had taken care of so many sick and dying.

And she had her own hardships, her own losses. He'd misjudged her. Underestimated her. What strength she had. What kindness.

He hadn't resisted the sudden urge to take her fingers in his. Smaller and more fragile, her hand fit in his palm.

She was as soft as spring rain, that sweet drizzle that made the leaves bud and the grass grow and the flowers dare to bloom. When he touched her, that's how she affected him. As if there was hope for him. For the permanent winter in his soul.

And he knew better.

That's why he placed her hand gently on the rail and turned away, strangely aching, and searched the waters for those elusive dolphins.

He did not touch her again.

As the girl behind the cash register handed her a pastry and a steaming tall raspberry mocha with whipped cream in a pretty paper cup, Kirby had to wonder. Had she done or said something to upset Sam?

After paying for their food, he turned and walked away from her without a single word. Not "I'll find us a table" or "That muffin sure looks good." Nothing polite or casual.

He'd joked with her this morning and during the first part of the ferry ride, but now he was distant and silent. Had she offended him in some way?

Maybe she ought to add this to her list of desirable characteristics: does not act in a confusing manner.

Kirby balanced the big cup of coffee and her enormous croissant on a pretty stoneware plate and followed Sam. He was already seated, his coat slung over the back of the empty chair beside him. He gathered the croissant egg-and-cheese sandwich with both hands and bit into it like a starving man.

"Sorry, I should have waited," he apologized

when she joined him, "but I'm half-dead with hunger. Ready to drop at any minute. You'd have to administer a coffee IV straight into my arm to revive me."

"Don't rely on me. I'm just as hungry and exhausted as you are. I'm ready to fall face first onto my plate."

"You look about as beat as I feel."

"I think the adrenaline is wearing off." She reached for her double mocha. Espresso slid over her tongue and down her throat. Yep, that was just what she needed.

"If heaven has a bakery, then this one is it," he said between bites. "It's good to know there will be pastry in the afterlife."

Kirby took a bite of her cheese croissant. Buttery flakes fell apart on her tongue, crepe thin and sheer perfection. As exquisite as the food was, she was more drawn to the man across the table.

There was a serious side to this man who liked to make her laugh. A very serious side.

"The view is amazing, too," he said as he dug in to his second croissant sandwich.

Kirby's tension drained away at the soft lull of the waves on the shore below, just outside the window. A beautiful place. The beach was rocky, and evergreens grew right up to the shore. The waning sunlight gleamed like polished glass on the moody gray waves. A big white-and-green ferry, the same one they'd ridden in on, honked long and loud, then eased away from the dock, loaded with cars and passengers headed toward Seattle.

"It must be a nice way to live. To commute by ferry." She tried to imagine it for herself, but couldn't. She wouldn't want to live anywhere but in Montana.

"This is the view I kept in my head when I needed to remember why I thought joining the army was a good idea. When I was being shot at. I used to tell myself I would come here, when I retired, and live near the water in peace."

"Did you?"

"Not the peace part."

"Do you think you'll be happy in a small town in Montana?" Kirby looked around her, at the bustling city and its inviting skyscrapers and every entertainment under the sun— theater and universities and museums.

"I have a helicopter. I can fly anywhere I want. I like Montana. It has a lot of good qualities I wouldn't trade for anything. Like wide-open spaces. Sincere people. Clean air. A quiet neighborhood."

"The downside is moving in next to me."

"I'll suffer through, somehow. Except one thing is going to be intolerable, and I might as well get it off my chest now. If we're going to be neighbors, I don't think I can take much more of this."

"Of what?" She looked sincere, caring and concerned. As if she would fix whatever it was, if she could.

It was wrong to tease her, but he couldn't help it. She brought out the worst in him. "There's this odor wafting over the fence."

"Are you saying my yard stinks?"

"That's what I'm saying, and it's only going to get worse when those long green stem things start to bloom. If I see one rose peeking over the fence into my yard, I'm going to kill it. Deadhead it right there. I'm a man, and I have a man's yard and I'm not putting up with dainty little roses peeking over the fence to mock me." He winked and polished off the last of his sandwich.

There was the Sam she knew and liked. Glad he was no longer so quiet and distant, she did her best to rise to the occasion. "Why, will a few pretty flowers diminish your value as a man?"

"Absolutely. Leo and I don't do flowers. Unless I forget to pull weeds and they bloom."

"That's too bad. I was going to offer you some of my cuttings. Oh, and I have the cutest little stepping stones. I have extra, if you'd like them."

"Please. Stepping stones. What I need is a big hammock. Maybe an extra refrigerator on the deck so I don't have to go inside to grab a soda."

"Plus, it will be handy when you have your band members and biker-gang friends over for a backyard music jam."

"Good idea." He was really starting to like her. It had been a long time since a woman had come along who could make him laugh.

This was the problem with getting to know someone. At first glance, she looked a certain way and he could make assumptions about how she was. If he hadn't been with her through the night and into this morning, he would have thought she was like one of those perfect girls on TV sitcoms, the kind that had no real troubles. Not ones that couldn't be resolved in thirty minutes, anyway.

That wasn't Kirby. He was close enough to see the faint lines in the corners of her eyes and by her mouth made by sadness. The furrows in her brow that told him she had plenty of worries. She had known sorrow.

Yet she was strong and self-sufficient. She had her own house, her own car and a nursing degree. In her spare time she saved little girls' lives, and when she smiled it was a wholesome beauty he saw. The genuine thing.

It wasn't so easy not to care about her now.

He stared at the window, troubled. The lap of water on the shore, an eternal rhythm, one from the start of time, should have by all rights comforted him.

It didn't.

He felt flawed next to her. A wounded soul who was too tarnished to be near her. The food in his mouth turned to sand and he stood and pushed out of his chair.

He walked away without an explanation. Left his jacket and his wallet on the table, and his coffee steaming. Kirby watched him with big startled eyes as he pushed out the door and into the cool wind from off the water.

He stood at the shoreline and let the wind

beat at him and the sound of the restless water pull at him until it subdued all the pain.

Did she approach him? Or did she wait for him to come back on his own? She had no clue what to do as she hesitated on the steep bank. The wind kicked up and she shivered.

He looked so alone as the storm rolled in, a solitary figure surrounded by a world of gray. He stood like a warrior of old, feet apart, spine straight, shoulders back, head up, as the rain came in a fine curtain of darker gray.

Well, he certainly couldn't stand out here in this weather without a coat. As if the elements had decided for her, Kirby tripped down the rocky slope, careful not to spill the coffees she held or drop the bakery sack or her heavy shoulder bag.

Behind her, car tires whispered on the damp pavement and a few shoppers dashed to their parked vehicles, splashing through the already building puddles. Women chatted through the wind and rain as they unlocked their SUVs. The world around her felt normal and connected.

And the man on the beach was set apart. Alone. Isolated.

Sad. That's how he seemed to her as she

waded toward him through the shifting dirt
and rocks beneath her sneakers. The water,
as gray as the clouds and as pensive, lapped
at his boots. He was wet from the rain.

"Sam?" She wasn't sure he'd heard her over
the growing storm. She stepped closer.

He had to have heard her, but he remained
as still as a statue. She could feel his pain like
the rain on her skin. "Sam?"

"Yeah. I know. The ferry's getting ready to
leave. Guess we should go."

He sounded distant, as if he wasn't really
there. Overhead thunder crashed, a metallic
sound that rumbled through the clouds for
miles, echoing like gunfire.

He closed his eyes, swiped his hand over
his face, wiping away the wet drops from the
rain. He looked ghost pale, and his eyes were
so dark, it was as if he'd shuttered his heart
and soul completely.

He wasn't okay, and she hurt for him. With
him.

As if he were dead inside, he took the coat
she offered and shrugged into it. He didn't
bother to zip up as the wind lashed him. She
pressed a coffee cup into his hand.

"Are you too good to be true?"

"Hardly. I had selfish motivations."

"You, selfish?"

"Sure. I figure if I have another double latte, that will be enough caffeine to keep me awake until we get back home."

"And you wanted the pilot to have a double shot, too."

"Triple, just in case you were sleepy. You look tired."

"I'm always tired—don't worry about it. And I've flown birds more tired than this and lived to tell the tale. Between the demanding special ops I flew and the worry over them before and after, I lived on adrenaline."

"Well, live on caffeine and keep us safe."

"Yes, ma'am." He saluted her.

"Special ops, huh? I can't believe they trusted you with an expensive helicopter. Don't those cost like millions of dollars? And they let *you* on board one?"

"On board? I got to fly those babies. Oh, yeah. I flew a Pave Low. Any target, any place and back."

"So piloting our medical flight has to be

pretty boring for you, when you're used to flying in danger."

"I've had enough danger to last me a lifetime. I'm content enough with a quiet life, and the chance to do some good. Which reminds me, has that little phone of yours rung?"

She dug it out of the inside pocket in her bag and squinted at the screen. "Nope. No message. I'll give Jeremiah a call once we're in the terminal."

"Yeah. I sure hope that little girl will be all right."

"Me, too." She had to walk fast to keep up with his long-legged stride. "The chance to do some good, huh? You can't be as bad as you make yourself out to be."

"I'm bad to the bone." He winked, far too cocky, but she didn't miss the shadow in his eyes, the sadness in his voice, the way he pulled away from her, keeping his distance.

From her? Or from anyone?

Who was this man? At first she'd thought he was a plumber, then a volunteer pilot. Now he was a lost soul, shrouded with rain.

What had brought him into her life? She couldn't help asking the question as he led the way down the sidewalk and to the covered walkway into the terminal. The commuter traffic had dwindled, so there were just the two of them on the quiet section of the ferry where Sam chose a seat.

He stared out the rain-smeared window and felt a dozen light years away.

Chapter Six

"My dear boy, you are coming to Sunday dinner," Aunt Ruth said, and it was not a question. That was a command if he'd ever heard one.

"Let me think about it. I may have to be out at the office tomorrow. Someone has to keep things running smoothly."

"I know you've got your hands full between running that airport and repairing the house, but it's Sunday—you should rest."

"Fine, fine, I'll be there. What's in it for me?"

Ruth's chuckle filled the cordless phone's receiver. "Food, nutritious food, that's what. I know you bachelors don't take time to cook a decent meal."

"Why cook when there's takeout?"

"On Sunday! We'll have home cooked, and I'm taking no prisoners—isn't that the saying? You'd better be here and I mean it." Enjoying her new role as the commander, Ruth wished him a good night and broke the connection.

His fondness for her remained, warm and certain. It was good to have family ties. Someone to fuss over him. To care for him.

And cook for him. He sure liked the sound of that.

His gaze drifted to the window, where Kirby's house was visible in the warm rain. A nap had cleared his sleep-deprived mind, but it hadn't driven away the confusion.

He'd sure had fun talking with her this morning. She made him laugh. And for a little while he hadn't felt alone. How wrong was that? He *had* to be alone. There was no other choice.

When he'd buried Carla, he'd given up on relationships. He didn't have the strength to go through that again. People hid their deep flaws and showed the good stuff. And that could cause a whole lot of heartache.

What about Kirby? Well, she was the shining exception. He'd expected her to be less than she appeared, but she was more. She'd opened up to him and shown him a part of her she kept private.

Okay, she was still too good to be true, right? She had to be, because he wasn't about to start questioning everything again.

It was easier just to keep his heart closed, and all the loss and pain and vulnerability that went with it. Closed off tight and locked out of sight. To accept the lessons he'd learned from Carla. The goodness in a person was not stronger than the bad. His hard-won philosophy of life.

A philosophy he'd tried to put aside this morning on the rainy beach, and couldn't.

He swore the rain had followed them all the way from Seattle. He'd kept ahead of the weather by the skin of his teeth, flying low and fast. Once they'd touched down on Montana soil, Kirby had gone her way, and he his.

He'd been exhausted, and so had she. Maybe that's why they hadn't spoken on the return flight or as she walked away from him in the parking lot in search of her car.

He'd thought about her all day.

There she was, zipping along the street in her car. Pulling into the driveway with the same careful grace she did everything. Her hair was yanked back into a ponytail, the way he liked it, and shone like burnished gold. Amazing.

Why had she gotten beneath his skin?

Oh, that was an easy answer. Because she was beautiful, smart, capable and compassionate. Not your average, everyday, run-of-the-mill kind of woman.

Well, he couldn't stand around thinking about her all day. It was late enough that there was no sense driving down to the office. Maybe he'd start work on patching the numerous and varied holes in the walls from the previous tenant.

He had a lot of work to do before he'd have this house the way he wanted it. New paint, new fixtures, new windows, a new furnace. He even planned on rewiring.

He was halfway down the stairs to the basement, where his tools and supplies were, when Leo's happy bark resounded through the house. The floorboards overhead groaned with the force of his weight as the dog ran from bedroom to front door. He sounded like a herd of charging dragons, breathing fire and in serious need of claw trimmings.

Whoever was on his step and about to ring the bell had better not be Ruth. He didn't want her seeing what had happened to her house. Not until he had it patched, painted and polished, anyway. He dashed back up the steps, already plotting ways to keep her from crossing the threshold, when the dulcet music of the old doorbell echoed through the house.

Leo went nuts, bouncing off the windowsill and howling with delight. He was more gentlemanly around Ruth, so that meant only one woman could be standing on their front step.

"Calm down, boy." Not surprised at all, he saw *her* through the glass.

Kirby McKaslin, protected by a cheerful red raincoat, smiled up at him from beneath the oversize hood. Fatigue darkened the skin beneath her eyes, but she sure looked good. The freckles on her nose stood out, probably because she wasn't wearing any makeup. He liked those freckles. They made her look beyond cute. Endearing.

He grabbed Leo by the collar and opened the door.

The rottweiler lunged, thrilled beyond his doggy self-control apparently. It took a second order for him to sit still, the way a gentleman, even a young and eager one, should.

"Look what blew onto my front porch,"

Sam said. "A pretty lady carrying what looks like food."

"Looks like." She gestured to the bulging white sack she cradled in one arm and to a cardboard drink tray. "I've come bearing good news and doughnuts."

"You've said the magic password—doughnut. You may enter." He held wide the door for her, hearing the old furnace wheeze on in a pathetic attempt to warm them. A failed attempt.

And it was a good thing he had a fire going in the fireplace, because it looked as if Kirby was shivering. Cold and tired. He knew how that felt, so he moved close.

She smelled like apples and cinnamon and rain. The curled ends of her ponytail brushed his knuckles as he helped her out of her raincoat. The fabric rustled, a couple of rain droplets tapped to the bare hardwood floor and he felt terrified and excited and alive all at once.

Exactly the same way he'd felt when he'd taken his first night-flight. Adrenaline-pumping, mind-racing speed through the darkness.

Wow. He hung her coat off the back of the wooden chair—the only furniture in the room—near the hearth. His hands shook so hard he nearly dropped the garment twice. What was that? What was she doing to him?

"Sit. Get warm." Did that sound like an order? He cleared his throat. Only then did he notice she held something else. A bright pink leash, and it was attached to her dog's collar.

How could he have not noticed she'd brought her cocker spaniel? It just went to show how much she affected him.

"Hello there, little one." He knelt to welcome Jessie.

The little dog came up to him politely and nudged his hand, eager to be petted. A sweet girl, like her owner.

"I almost hated to ring the bell. I was afraid you were sleeping. But with the way Leo was barking even before I reached the porch, I figured I might as well. Who could sleep through that racket?" Kirby leaned to unsnap her dog's leash and laughed when Leo swiped his tongue across her face in an ambush kiss.

"You're an awful popular lady in these parts," he told her as he grabbed Leo's collar. He sent the rottweiler to the kitchen, and watched as the gentle cocker spaniel waddled after him. A few seconds later he heard the unmistakable sound of dogs crunching on dog food.

"Does this mean they're best friends?" Kirby asked.

"It must be. Friends share food. I think it's a rule. And speaking of food." He couldn't hold off another second, so he grabbed the bakery bag. Just what he thought. The sweet fragrance of doughnut, chocolate and custard made his knees weak. "Darlin', you have made my day."

"I thought you might like 'em."

"I was bummed because I didn't go back in that bakery and get myself some chocolate doughnuts to go. You remembered."

"I couldn't resist. Besides, anyone who gets up in the middle of the night to fly a sick child across two states deserves to have a custard-filled doughnut."

He couldn't believe her thoughtfulness. How could he doubt it? The proof was in his hands. "You are my favorite person ever."

"I'm glad. Hey, give me one of those. I've been dying to try them, but I didn't sneak even a tiny bite. I waited to share them with you."

"I guess this means we're like our dogs."

"We are?" A quick flash of confusion, and then she beamed, all soft golden beauty. "We're friends. Yes, I think we are. Whether we like it or not."

"We'll just have to suffer through the doughnuts and a friendship. Sad." He held out the bag and offered her first choice.

"Terrible. I think I can put up with you for a friend," she said as she chose the top doughnut and wrapped it in a napkin because it was pretty sticky. "If you pay me enough."

"Sorry, I've already got my budget for this month set. I'll put you down for next month?"

"Perfect. I'll wait to be friendly to you then. My offer of pastries is null and void." Why did she love teasing him so much? "Give me back that doughnut."

"Too late. Sorry." He bit down, and his eyes rolled back in his head. He moaned deep in his throat. "Oh, that's good."

"It's only a doughnut," she said, and bit into hers. Chocolate delighted her tongue. The crisp cake was sweet as sugar, and the rich creamy custard filling made her eyes water. It *was* so good.

"Did I tell you? When I die, I'm saying to

St. Peter, 'I tried really hard to be good. Now, where are the doughnuts'?"

She laughed and helped herself to a cup of coffee, a warm latte that chased the last of the chill from her bones. "Oh, I heard from Jeremiah."

"How's little Sarah?"

"She's improving, but still serious. It's been hard, because she needs a bone-marrow transplant to get well, but no one in her family is a match."

"She has to wait for a donor match?"

"Yes, and who knows how long that will take?" Sometimes there was so little she could do, Kirby felt useless.

Sam stared into the dying fire. "Little kids shouldn't have to be sick."

"I agree. It's sad. All things have their seasons and their reasons—isn't that the saying? Maybe it will soon be Sarah's season to get well." She hoped it with all her heart.

Sam grabbed a chunk of split wood from the pile off to the side of the hearth. He was a big and strong man, a little rough looking and unpolished, but what a good heart he must have. What trials, she wondered, had he endured?

She remembered Ruth's words. *He's had a*

hard life, the poor man. What had happened to him?

He knelt before the fire, pushed back the screen and placed the logs into the flames. Maybe it was the way the dancing light, golden and glowing, haloed him. Burnished the fall of his short hair and gilded his impressive strength.

What a man. Kirby felt as if she'd been lifted out of her chair and onto a cloud. She'd never felt like this before. Weightless and tingling and happy.

Unaware, he grabbed the iron poker and nudged the newly burning pieces of wood into place "What about you? What's the story on Kirby McKaslin? My inquiring mind wants to know."

"Inquiring? What about you? I'm much more interested in you."

"We've talked about me. I told you lots of stuff this morning. Now it's your turn."

"I'm boring. There's nothing to tell."

"Sure there is. Why aren't you married, or at least engaged?"

"I'm not going to tell you about my interpersonal disasters."

"Hit a nerve, did I?" He hung the utensil on the hook in the brick wall and stole the last chocolate frosted doughnut from the bag. "Was he your high school sweetheart?"

"No, was yours?"

"We're talking about you, remember?" He sat on the floor and got comfortable. "Are you too chicken to answer my question?"

"No. Embarrassed." She ran her fingertip around the edge of her coffee cup. Did she tell him? If he were interested in her, then how could she withhold the truth? "I'm not married because no one's ever asked me."

"No one? Nope, I don't believe it. How could someone like you never have a relationship get that serious?"

"What do you mean, someone like me?" Her eyes widened, and in those deep blue irises Sam saw the real Kirby. So vulnerable and alone.

Just like him.

Did she fear he'd hurt her about this? "You are good and kind. You have your own house and a good job. Why wouldn't a good man want you?"

Her gaze clouded and she looked away. Her mouth curled down and she frowned.

He'd said the wrong thing. Well, he could fix that. He'd keep talking until he said something right. "You have a lot to offer a man."

"Equity and a good paycheck?" She tried to make it a joke, but couldn't quite do it.

"No, I meant you are a woman with a lot going for her. You've proven you work hard and honestly. You have a caring heart. And you're beautiful. Do you know that?"

She stared hard into the bottom of her coffee cup. "You're my friend. You have to say nice things."

"I'm not your friend yet, remember? You're not on the budget until next month."

She blinked hard. Took another sip of coffee.

"Tell me the real reason you aren't married," he asked again.

The honest one, she knew he meant. Her vision was still a little blurry, so she blinked again, trying to focus. In case Sam was interested in her, he might as well know how she felt. "Because I don't want to settle. I want to marry the right man for me. He has to be out there somewhere, don't you think? My soul mate. My one true love."

"You believe in true love?"

It sounded corny. She knew. But that didn't mean it was impossible. True love did happen. Her older sister Karen had found it. Plenty of friends she knew had found their someone special.

"I was like you once." Sam sounded thoughtful as he got up and paced the room. The old floorboards creaked and groaned beneath his weight as he moved.

"*You* believed in true love?"

"I found mine. Married her. Our wedding day was the happiest of my life. I thought she was a good-hearted person who loved me, but I was wrong. She married for financial security and not for love. She wanted to be an officer's wife. A pilot's wife."

"You're divorced?"

He stopped at the window. "No. I'm a widower."

A widower? She felt so sad for him. No wonder he kept her at arm's length. It all made sense now. His distance had nothing to do with her. "Is there anything I can do?"

He shook his head, staring out the window, his throat working, muscles bunching in his jaw.

Outside the rain pummeled down, and the house resounded with the noise of it battering the roof and punching against the siding.

A thousand drumming sounds echoing in

the big, empty rooms, and all that noise was unable to diminish the silence of one man's sorrow.

Through the evening and into the next day Kirby thought of Sam's confession and his sorrow.

She had driven home to the ranch, where growing wheat had turned the fields a lush emerald green. Mom had made a roast, and Karen brought the rest. Scalloped potatoes and baked beans and rolls and a salad. Gramma brought a double batch of her beloved chocolate chocolate-chip cookies.

For years, family gatherings hadn't been the same. Allison would be forever missing. Her pictures still hung on the wall, the yearly school pictures from kindergarten to graduation. Kirby was glad to get home, where the loss didn't seem so huge. Or her failures.

Being back home again only made her wonder about Sam. His house was a constant reminder. It was hard not to notice it through her windows as she dusted and vacuumed. Harder still when she headed outside to weed her flower beds. Jessie ran around the backyard, tailing butterflies that flew just out of her reach or trying to befriend the squirrels that lived in the trees and stared curiously down at her.

The hum of an engine and the hush of tires on concrete rose over the fence. Sam was back from his aunt's. She straightened to give her back a rest. The engine died and the truck door rasped open.

"Out, Leo. C'mon." Sam's deep chuckle sounded over the thud of the big dog landing on the concrete drive. The door slammed, and master and dog headed inside and stayed there.

All afternoon she thought of the man next door and remembered his sorrow.

As she was lifting the take-and-bake pizza from the oven, she heard a familiar rap on her front door. Jessie raced through the house, barking in heartfelt greeting. The door squeaked open. Which sister had arrived first?

"Hello, little one." Karen. So she had made it. Now that she was married and expecting, she didn't have quite so much time to spend with her sisters. But that was understandable.

The hinges squeaked again as another sister walked in. This one didn't knock, so it could only be her littlest sister. Michelle tapped through the house in her latest shoe purchase and dumped two six-packs of soda on the counter.

"Perfect timing." Kirby rolled the pizza cutter through the gooey cheese and doughy crust. "You've got that look on your face. What's up with you?"

"I can't wait a second more. I've got to know." Michelle abandoned her purse and keys and leaned on tiptoe to get the best view of Sam's backyard through the window over the kitchen sink.

"What are you doing?"

"I've heard all the gossip down at the Snip & Style. But gossip isn't reliable. Nobody has actually met him. But you, sister dear, had to have at least said howdy to your handsome neighbor."

Kirby circled around her sister, who was blocking the path to the dishwasher, and nudged her aside so she could open the door and drop the utensil inside. "I've said hi to him."

"Hi? It's gotta be more than that. Someone flew with him to Seattle."

Kirby put the soda in the refrigerator to stay cold. "Sam's my neighbor, nothing more."

"Then can I have him?" Michelle was

young and impressionable enough to believe true love could be around every corner and saw no shame in openly looking for it.

"Help yourself, but he's probably not your type."

"Oh, it's like that, is it?" Karen asked as she opened the cupboards. "You have your eye on him."

"No. He's not my type, either, I think." Unless she wanted to marry a good-hearted, successful, hero of a man who was kind and funny and intelligent. "Besides, I know for a fact he's not looking for a relationship."

"Ooh! You got shot down." Michelle's eyes widened, and she snapped around, determined to know all. "Was it during the flight to Seattle, or back? Did you two have a chance to talk? Did he kiss you?"

Kirby thought of Sam's firm mouth on hers, and knew his kiss would be incredible. But she had no chance of ever knowing, since he'd made it clear he wasn't looking for a wife. "We're neighbors, nothing more."

"That's wise." Kendra walked into the conversation with a Tupperware tub of Gramma's cookies and the Monopoly box. "It takes a long time to get to know a person, and when you're considering a serious relationship with someone, you need to be careful."

Michelle was back at the window. "Ooh, there he is now. He looks really nice. He must work out to be in that great shape."

"I wouldn't know." Kirby joined in as she set the table.

"Why don't you run next door and invite him over? We all could just sneak back out the way we came. You've got pizza and soda. Men like pizza and soda."

"Michelle, stop! Sam is nice, but he's not the one meant for me."

"How can you be so sure?"

"Because I am." Was this how it was going to be all evening? With her sisters trying to pressure her over a man who wouldn't want her?

Kendra opened the box and started setting up. "Don't worry, Kirby, I'm on your side. Love takes time. Or it should. You can't get carried away by emotions and the whirlwind of first love. You have to make sure he's the right man for you."

Kirby's throat tightened, because she knew that not all men were what they seemed. No one knew that more than Kendra. "I feel safe with him. He's strong, but he's protective."

"Ooh, nice." Michelle changed windows so she could keep watching Sam in the backyard with his dog. "The right man is out there somewhere. He sure looks like the right man. Does he like you, Kirby? You know, does he give you 'the look'?"

"No, he doesn't." And for a good reason. Kirby didn't feel right revealing Sam's secrets, and that's all she said as she headed to the stove. "Michelle, you go first."

"All right, all right." Michelle abandoned her view out the window and grabbed a plate. "I think Kirby's sweet on her hunky pilot next door. What do you think, Kendra?"

"I think she's wise taking it slow."

"Thank you, sis."

"I say, take your time," Karen added as she filled glasses with ice. "If it's true love, then it will happen the way it's meant to."

"What are you saying to do? Wait around and see what happens?" Michelle complained as she filled her plate with pizza. "Oh, c'mon. Kirby, you're almost thirty and still single. After thirty, isn't it like really hard to find a husband? All the good ones are already married."

"Believe what you want. I say a good man is hard to find at any age." Kendra paused as she counted out the Monopoly money. "The real question is, what kind of man is Sam at heart? Down deep, to the soul?"

Exactly what I was wondering, Kirby thought. Sam was rough around the edges and bold and definitely not what she would have pictured as the perfect man. But she could feel his heart.

He didn't feel the same way about her. He didn't feel *her* heart. It was as simple as that.

They were neighbors. They were friendly. They each had their separate paths in life.

That was simply the way it was.

"All right, get your pizza. We've got a game to play." Michelle headed for the table. "Karen, it's your turn to roll first. Which token did you want?"

There was no more time to wonder about Sam Gardner. Besides, the issue was settled. He was not her Mr. Right.

More sad than she wanted to admit, Kirby grabbed four sodas from the fridge and joined her sisters at the table where girl talk, good food and their favorite board game awaited.

The constant tap of the rain was a companion that at least kept the silence at bay.

In the year and a half since Carla's death, he'd first hated the loneliness. He'd been grieving her, and being alone in their house had been horrible. He'd asked for more work and had hired a real estate agent to sell the house.

Time had healed a lot of the sorrow, so now when he was alone he appreciated the silence. Appreciated the peace and quiet.

Carla had been a desperately unhappy person beneath the soft smiles and sweet face. When life put hardships in her way, there had been no steel in her. Only anger. Why didn't she have a better house, a new car and a better husband?

He'd done his best, but in the end he'd learned you can't make another person happy. No matter how hard you try, how much you bend. He'd loved Carla. He'd given her everything he had. It hadn't been enough for her.

It had taken time and his pastor's wise advice for him to realize that he'd been good to her. She'd been his wife, and he'd cherished her even when she was difficult and angry. But her unhappiness came from inside her. In the end there was nothing he could do to help her. Or to save her.

And so he'd appreciated the tranquillity

of a quiet evening by himself. Without her constant criticism or her complaining or her angry comments. There was nothing poking at him, tearing at him. There was just him and Leo, and peace.

Until tonight.

Sam opened the back door and whistled, and the dog bounded through the rain, skidded on the wet back deck and careened into the house. Sam shut the door just in time to get sprayed by rainwater as Leo planted himself on all fours and shook.

"Hey, quit that." Laughing, Sam grabbed a box of treats from the top shelf. "Sit. Good boy."

He tossed the jumbo-sized dog biscuit into the air and Leo leaped, retrieved it and ran off to crunch on his treat in private.

Sam took his tools downstairs. He'd had a productive afternoon and evening. He'd patched the many holes in every room, and in a few days he'd be able to sand and prep to paint. It was a good feeling. The house was going to look sharp when he was finished.

Once his tools were tucked away in the workroom, he started locking up. He pulled the blind on the back door's window on the way through the kitchen. Then when he went to tug the sheet into place over the kitchen window—he needed to replace that window before he installed a shade—he naturally looked outside to the square of light shining so brightly.

Kirby's kitchen window. There she was with her back to him, seated at the round table in the kitchen with three other women, who looked remarkably like her. They had to be sisters. The same golden-blond hair, the same slope of nose and chin.

Playing Monopoly. Talking and laughing. There was a bowl of popcorn between them and soda cans at each woman's elbow. One sister rolled the dice and reached across the table to move her token.

Kirby and the other sisters exchanged looks of agony while one sister shot her fist into the air. Sam watched transfixed as Kirby counted out her play money and handed it over to the winning sister.

Too good to be true? If this wasn't proof enough, what would be? On a Sunday night, after a weekend of volunteering on a medical flight to save a critically ill child and going to church, Kirby McKaslin wasn't out partying or socializing or doing anything nefarious.

No, she was playing a board game with her

sisters. He wouldn't be surprised if this is how she spent *every* Sunday night.

How much had he changed over the years, he wondered? That he could look a good person in the face and no longer see it? No longer believe it?

He felt tarnished and unworthy and weary. And wrong.

Ashamed, he drew the makeshift curtain into place and flicked out the light. Walked through the dark living room, the fire now only a faint glow of embers in the fireplace, to his room. He read much of the night, so he didn't have to think of Kirby.

Chapter Seven

The coffee shop was busy when Kirby dropped by on her way to the hospital. She was working swing tonight. While she was grateful for the work and the paycheck, she'd be glad when her new job started. Only a few more days now.

"Do you need some help?" Kirby asked her sister, who was two customers deep and working fast behind the industrial-sized espresso machine.

"No, I've got it. Go sit down and I'll bring you a mocha."

"You're a doll. Thanks." Kirby gratefully sank into a chair in the corner and let the sunshine warm her.

"You look troubled," Karen said a few minutes later after the minirush of customers had been cared for. She set two drinks on the cloth-covered table. A double mocha with extra chocolate sprinkles. And a glass of lemonade.

Kirby took a long pull of the hot, wonderful coffee. That's what she needed. Caffeine and comfort all rolled into one. "How are you two holding up?"

"We're great." Karen's left hand covered her growing stomach, the diamonds in her rings sparkling happily in the sunlight. Her touch to her belly was one of love for the little one due in only three months. "Tired, and my feet are killing me, and she's kicking me pretty hard. But those are little things. I have so much to be grateful for. A healthy baby and a wonderful husband."

"And a new house. How's the unpacking going?"

"Slow, but sure. Zach's got his workshop all unpacked and set up, and me? I've hardly done anything. This morning I had to hunt around in the boxes stacked in the garage for the box of extra towels. What can I say? It's been an adventure."

An adventure. She'd never quite thought of marriage as that before. Of the journey of it. It had always meant to her the end of a long road of looking for the right man to marry. "You look happy."

"I am." Karen glowed from deep inside and it showed in her smile, in her eyes, in her voice. In the contentment that seemed to radiate from her like light from the sun.

"How have you done it?" Kirby opened her journal to keep her hands busy. She hated talking about what had happened that day they lost their sister. "How have you found peace?"

"I only had to grieve her loss. I wasn't the one who almost died with her."

Kirby squeezed her eyes shut, as if to keep the hurt from welling up and spilling over. "I wasn't that hurt."

"I was there at the hospital, remember? Gramma and I sat by your bedside and refused to move."

I remember. Kirby wished she could wipe away the memory and the pain from her soul. Everyone had said to let it go, to release the pain so that peace could enter her heart.

And she had. But the guilt remained. The guilt that she had lived. That she was here alive and well, when her sister wasn't. How did she let go of the guilt? "Sunday nights will never be the same without Allison."

"I know, but we have each other. We love each other, and we still love Allison. That doesn't have to change. You don't have to be afraid."

Kirby's eyes flew open. How did Karen know? "I'm not afraid."

"We all are. Life is a journey, with ups and down, good experiences and bad. That's the way it is." Karen reached out to brush Kirby's bangs out of her eyes. "Did I tell you Zach and I settled on a name for the baby? We're going to call her Allison."

"Good choice." Kirby's eyes burned, and she blinked hard. "Our sister would be glad."

"Glad? She's probably signing up to be her guardian angel as we speak." Karen's gentle chuckle was a good sound. A hopeful one. "We're not alone, Kirby. You're not alone."

"I know."

"I hate to see you so unhappy. I think you ought to stop working so hard. Now that you're finished with your master's, you need to schedule in some fun time. Maybe some dating time?"

"I'm not going to date Sam Gardner. Stop. I thought you were on my side. Don't turn into Michelle on me."

"I *am* on your side. Always." The bell above the door jangled as more customers crowded in from the blustery May day. "Oops. Gotta go."

Kirby sipped her coffee, opened a book to read.

A folded piece of notepaper used as a bookmark caught her eye. That paper sure looked familiar. It was the lavender stationery she liked so well.

Across the top she'd scrawled in glittery purple gel pen, "My One True Love."

It was her list for the perfect man. She'd written it last winter. It had been right before Christmas and she'd been making Christmas and birthday lists, since her birthday was in December. Why not make up a list for what she truly wanted? she'd rationalized at the time.

"A faithful man. Handsome. Kind. Handsome. Has a great job. Handsome."

Had she really written that? She blushed, embarrassed. Looks were important, but she'd made it sound as if it was the most important part. Pleasing looking, that would be better, she decided, and dug a pen out of her purse. She crossed out all those *handsome*s.

That left only three more attributes.

"Honest. Loves animals and children. Will love me, anyway."

Where was she going to find a man like that?

As if fate had heard her and tapped her on the shoulder, she looked up and there he was on the street outside. Climbing out of his pickup and tugging his baseball cap lower to shade his eyes from the bright sun.

Leo bounded out of the truck, too. Obedient and well trained when he wanted to be, the big dog stuck to Sam's side as they made their way along the sidewalk and disappeared into Corey's Hardware.

Sam. Her heart rose until she felt as if her entire being were floating somewhere near the ceiling. And how was that possible, when she was clearly sitting very firmly in the chair? How could one man affect her so much? And why?

He wasn't interested in her. He didn't look at her that way, the way a man did when he was truly interested.

Or did he?

Either way, her time was up. She'd better get going so she wouldn't be late for her last day of work. Times had been so tough when she'd first decided to go back to graduate school, and slowly things had worked out. She'd found private nursing work, and then landed a swing shift at the hospital and had enough extra money to buy her own house. Her life was turning out fine.

Maybe this sadness she carried and the loneliness of being single would work out fine, too.

There was Sam again, striding with that easy athletic gait of his heading back from the hardware. A small bag in hand. Leo at his side. Unaware of her, he opened the door and waited for Leo to leap into the cab.

For one brief second he hesitated. Wind-blown and sun kissed and as handsome as temptation. Then his gaze swung toward her and stopped at her table. Could he see her? Did he know she was watching him?

His smile came slow and sweet. He saluted her before he climbed into his truck.

Kirby woke the next morning to blissful peace. Jessie was curled up in her little dog bed in the corner of the room, a soft bundle of golden curls and sweetness. It sure was nice having Sam for a neighbor. It was— Kirby squinted at her clock—11:06 a.m. and she'd slept straight through last night without a single outside noise loud enough to wake her.

Her last swing shift. Whew. Kirby rolled out of bed and pulled back the curtains. Dappled sunshine tumbled into the room with a warm, lemony cheer that made her feel as if this new phase of her life was going to start out just right.

She'd done a lot of volunteer work at the free clinic, to gain experience and because serving her community was what she was driven to do. Obligated. A quick flash of an image burst into her mind, of flame and broken metal and seat stuffing strewn in the grass—

No. I won't think of it. She'd vowed never to think of it again. Her fear and uncertainty lingered still.

She hauled her nightshirt over her head and stepped into the bathroom. She crossed in front of the counter-length mirror to grab a soft fluffy towel from the shelf and saw her reflection.

The scars of pink and red that splashed across her back and shoulders were an ugly, horrible reminder. She looked away and hung the towel on the wooden dowel next to the bathtub.

She'd been lucky. The scars didn't show, unless she wore a tank top in the summer, and she rarely did that anymore. How many times had she given thanks the scars weren't on her face? Or her hands? The burns had been slight compared to others—

You have a lot to be thankful for, Kirby Anne McKaslin. And she was thankful. But she felt guilty, too.

She was here when so many others were not.

And why was this bothering her so much? Oh, she knew the answer to that. Sam Gardner. He wasn't interested in her. He had problems and sorrow of his own. He wasn't interested in dating her.

And even if he *was* interested, what would he think of her scars?

What would he think of the ones he could not see?

Well, that settled it. She knew it would take a rare man—and maybe there never would be one—who could love her, anyway.

She turned the faucets and adjusted the water and vowed to put Sam Gardner out of her thoughts.

That vow lasted almost an entire hour and eighteen minutes. She was fertilizing the roses in her front flower beds against the house when she heard a pickup easing down the quiet street. She checked on her dog. Jessie was lying in the shade from the hedges and chewing on her favorite rawhide bone. Kirby recognized the big pickup slowing down.

Sam. He stopped in the middle of the empty street and his window slid downward. The dark glasses he wore accentuated the straight blade of his nose and the hard line of his jaw as he nodded to her. "Thought you were going to keep the noise down."

"I'm being too loud?"

"Sure. I thought we had an agreement. You keep your band members quiet, and I'll do the same with mine. But now it's no deal."

Jessie hopped up and ran with her bone to the sidewalk. She wagged her tail in greeting. Kirby dashed after her, just to make sure she stayed out of the street. "Jessie and I are just getting started with our loud and rowdy ways. Take it as fair warning."

"I'm so afraid. What are you girls doing?"

"Jessie is supervising while I play gardener."

"You girls have fun. The boy and I are going

to paint today." Sam tipped his hat, friendly, the same way he might treat any neighbor.

And that's what they were. Neighbors. Nothing more and nothing less. "Good luck," she called.

He waved as he pulled into his drive, then disappeared behind the tall hedge.

Now, how long can you go without thinking of him again? she thought. Forty-five minutes later she was rinsing out the bucket when Jessie woke up with a startled bark from her nap in the shade and ran off at top speed, her short little legs churning and her long flopping ears flying back in the wind.

"Hey!" Kirby took off after her, only to skid to a stop in the middle of the lawn.

Sam knelt in the middle of the sidewalk, looking fine in a pair of worn jeans and a black T-shirt that said Born To Fly. The dark material emphasized his rock-solid build. The wonderful, masculine look of him…

Don't look. That was the best solution, she thought as an awkward silence stretched between them. Jessie and Leo touched noses and wagged tails in greeting.

She broke the silence. "How's the painting going?"

"I got everything taped. I wanted to get

started, but the boy decided I should take him for a walk. He kept bringing me his leash and standing in the way. I figured it would be more productive to give in." With obvious affection Sam ran his hand over the dog's broad head. "I haven't seen you in a while. Where have you been hanging out?"

"I've had family and work obligations." She realized he hadn't mentioned yesterday in town, when he'd spotted her watching him through the coffee-shop window. Neither did she.

Another silence settled between them. Awkward feeling. This man in front of her was a different side of Sam. While he bantered with her, his joking lacked heart. He seemed different from the man she'd gotten used to laughing with. Different from the man she'd seen at his living-room window, staring into the rain.

"Want to come on a walk with us? Leo and I could use the company."

"Jessie has already had her walk."

"Really? Maybe she'd still like to take a spin around the block. How about it, Jess?" He knelt, and his big, rough-looking hands were kind as he stroked the top of her head.

He tilted his head, as if he were listening to her. "You do? Okay, I'll tell her."

He straightened, humor flickering in his dark eyes. "Jessie says that she'd love to go. She just needs her leash. Could you get that for her, please?"

"Aren't you funny?"

"I'm a comedian, remember? And I have a strange sympathetic relationship with dogs. I understand them. They understand me. It's a gift."

"I'll get her leash." Honestly. Was it her fault the dogs and the man next door had already made the decision? She had no other option than to grab the pink nylon rope from the front step, where she'd left it when she'd decided to let Jessie run in the yard unimpeded.

"What are you doing playing hooky?" she asked as she snapped the leash into place.

"The airport runs itself for the most part. That's the beauty of it. I can work when I need to, but take off when I want. What? Don't look at me like that."

"Like what?"

"Like you think I could be more industrious. I worked long and hard for twelve years in the military. The corporate job I had, I was never home. I figure after sixteen years of working nonstop, I've earned a little time when I want it."

"Hey, I didn't say you hadn't."

Leo took off with an eager lunge, and her polite cocker spaniel followed him. She tried to fall in step with Sam on the sidewalk. But he took off in a fast march like a soldier taking point.

"I've always wondered what you do in your spare time, when you're not saving sick kids or flying off on a mission of mercy. Now I know. You grow roses and walk your dog."

"Speaking of curiosity, everyone is wondering about the mysterious stranger come to town with his expensive new helicopter and the dog he takes just about everywhere."

"I have two choppers. A man needs his play toys to be happy."

"Oh, so you go up in the sky to play? Sure. Don't we all."

"What? You don't like flying?"

"I don't mind it except for the small fact that the ground is so far away."

Sam checked traffic at the curb, but Leo had already decided the coast was clear, touched his nose to Jessie's and protectively paraded across the street. He was a good dog. Sam felt no small bit of pride in that. Leo was his best friend, a companion to fill the loneliness of his life.

He would be forever grateful, because the truth was, he'd never consider marrying again.

Kirby knew that. Right? She wasn't looking at him in that way as she had when they'd first met. As if she were sizing him up as a potential suitor. Nope, she hardly even looked at him as she power-walked beside him, struggling to keep up. And he was holding Leo back, too.

"Slow down, boy." He chuckled when Leo tossed a questioning look over his shoulder. Yeah, he knew, they were going more slowly than their normal pace, but this was no normal walk. The little spaniel was wearing herself out.

It was companionable, even at what Sam considered a snail's pace. The shade from the trees lining the sidewalk was pleasant. The neighborhood was tidy, the cozy houses well kept and surrounded with picket fences and flowers and well-maintained lawns.

Peace. Contentment. He'd come a long way to find it, and had fought long and hard to be here. In this place in his life. He'd lived through hell and back in his career. He'd lost his heart in his marriage. He still had hope, and that's why he was here. Drinking in the soothing sunlight like water, letting it warm him. There were bad times, but the good ones always came. And they were all the sweeter.

Leo leaped across the street—there was no traffic, Sam knew, as he'd already checked—and off came the leash. With a hop and a bark the rottweiler took off at a dead run, then turned to look over his shoulder expectantly.

"I know, I'm not fast enough for you." Sam yanked the throw toy out of his jeans back pocket and hurled the orange bone hard. It flew end over end through the streaks of sunshine among the old maples ringing the children's play area and into the open green grass. Leo bounded in glee after it.

Kirby had knelt to unsnap her spaniel's leash. The polite little creature wagged her little stub of a tail, eager to join in the fun, but obedient. What gentleness, Sam thought, watching. Kirby ran her slim, sensitive fingers over her dog's back. "There you go. What a good girl you are."

The spaniel touched her nose to Kirby's in obvious adoration before she turned tail and leaped toward Leo, who was returning with the toy clamped between his powerful teeth.

Leo strutted, proud of his remarkable fetching skills.

"Can I pet the doggie?" A cute little girl about knee-high toddled away from the play area. Her mother came running up.

"He's good with kids," he told the woman.

Since Leo was a fan of receiving attention from adoring females, he sat and looked as handsome as possible while the little girl stroked her small hand down his front leg.

"His name is Leo and this is Jessie," Kirby said as she knelt beside Leo and showed the child how to caress the top of the dog's head.

Leo preened, trying to charm the watchful mother over. He was a ham for attention.

Sam leaned back against a solid tree trunk, contemplating his next-door neighbor. Her soft almost curly hair tumbled down her back and rose on the breeze and gleamed in the sun. Kirby McKaslin was the most enchanting woman he'd ever met.

And what chance did a man like him have of loving a woman like that?

The truth was, she wasn't going to love him in return.

He wouldn't want her to.

No. She deserved a whole lot more than he could ever give her. Longing shadowed her eyes and showed plainly on her face as she interacted with the little girl.

Sadness weighed him down and he took off, just to get away.

Marriage. Kids. It wasn't going to happen. His heart was cold and broken and in so many pieces, how could it ever be made whole again? And if it could, he'd never trust another woman. Not even this captivating lady with gentle, healing hands and the loveliest smile on earth.

Sitting in the quiet of her house on Sunday evening when the sunlight grew soft and pearled, she frowned at the numbers illuminated on the screen of her calculator. And retotaled her outstanding checks.

The hardest part about living in a small town was that a girl couldn't keep a secret. By week's end, Kirby was worn out from explaining to her sisters, her parents, her friends and to Jeremiah, during her Saturday-morning shift at the free clinic, that no, she wasn't dating Sam Gardner.

How had half the town spotted them at the small neighborhood park for what couldn't have been more than forty-five minutes? The dogs had played so well together, it was a sign, Michelle said. Karen wanted to know if she'd say yes if Sam happened to ask her out for dinner. Kendra said she'd heard good things through the grapevine about Sam.

He'd made good money as a corporate pilot and had invested his money well, Ruth Gardner had added at the gas station, when they both happened to be filling their tanks. He'd been hurt, and he needed a good woman to show him love was worth the risk.

Fine, but would that woman be her? Nope. Kirby wasn't going to pine after a man who didn't look at her in that way. Not lustful or anything like that—that wasn't what she meant. She wanted a husband who would love her as if she'd hung the moon, in spite of her flaws. A man who looked at her and saw his everything.

That certainly wasn't Sam. And if she was disappointed, well, she was an adult. She could handle it. She tried to keep faith that somewhere her one true love was waiting for her. When she fell in love, it would be with the right man, and it would be forever.

That's fine and dandy, Kirby, but this train

of thought isn't helping you balance your checkbook.

Well, short of a miracle, she wasn't going to find the $1.63 she was missing.

Someone knocked at her front door—probably Michelle—and Jessie woke with a start from her nap and dashed across the house, eagerly greeting whoever was walking right in. There was a rustle of paper and a tap of shoes on the entry tile.

"Hi there, cutie." It was Michelle.

After appropriately greeting the dog, Michelle bounded into the kitchen with a handful of helium balloons and a grocery sack. "Surprise! It's not every day a girl starts work at her very own practice."

"Hey, thanks." Kirby took the bunch of balloons thrust at her. Half a dozen orbs floated overhead and bounced against her stucco-covered ceiling. The sayings ranged from Congratulations! to You Go Girl! to Bon Voyage!

"I liked the colors," Michelle explained. "Karen's not coming tonight. She's too tired, and I told her to stay home and let her husband spoil her. There's always next week. Did she tell you about the baby's name? Isn't that awesome?"

"Yes." Kirby's throat ached as she anchored the balloons to the back of the closest kitchen chair.

Life moved on—it was the way of things. But it wasn't easy.

Why was she feeling so down today? So hopeless?

Because she knew what Michelle was going to say next, and she was tired. She was weary of wondering if every unmarried man she met was the one. She'd done this too many times, with exactly the same kind of outcome. When she'd first met Jeremiah on a medical flight he hadn't been seeing anyone. And she'd hoped, briefly, that he might be the man for her.

But, no, they hadn't had much in common besides their volunteer work, and he'd never once shown any interest in her.

And maybe it hit her so hard because she felt something different for Sam. She didn't merely see him. She *felt* him. Felt the sadness in his heart.

It was a connection that tugged at her like the earth at the moon, pulling her close and not letting her go. Even now, when she knew there was no chance, she still felt that invisible thread of her heart to his. All she had to do was look out the window and see him on his ladder, scraping off the paint from his house, and she ached.

I could love that man, deep and true and forever.

It hurt that he didn't want her. Didn't feel the same in return.

Michelle pulled the box of Scrabble from the bag she carried and began setting up at the kitchen table. Michelle had that look about her, but before she could say one word about Sam, Kendra burst through the door with a cake and a casserole. Kirby made sure the subject of Sam Gardner didn't come up in conversation that evening. Or haunt her thoughts as she lay awake staring at the wall until sleep finally claimed her.

Chapter Eight

Her first day at work had been a hard one. Good, but long. A strain of a virus with bronchitis was making its way through the local schools and communities. She made sure every patient who walked through the doors, appointment or not, was seen and treated before she locked up and headed home.

Her little bungalow had never looked so good as it did at the moment she pulled into her driveway. The bright sun welcomed her, dappling through the mature maple's broad green leaves over her house, over her. The colorful blush of the first roses peered shyly up at her as she dragged her tired feet along the walkway. The walkway where she'd first seen Sam Gardner.

There's no chance, Kirby. Forget it. Move

on, she told herself, and it was merely the truth. So why did a tiny piece of her heart keep wanting to hope?

She had to stop thinking about him. Otherwise, all she'd do was set herself up for more heartache.

Her dog's happy greeting went a long way toward reviving her dragging energy level. The balloons waved in the current from the heat register as she entered the kitchen. The bakery cake Kendra had brought over was on the corner of the island. Happy First Day was written in yellow icing on the half that remained.

It *had* been an excellent day. She felt satisfied, grateful for this job she knew she was going to love. Maybe she'd fire up the gas barbecue instead of cooking her hamburger inside. The evening was temperate, the warmest of the season so far. Inspired, Kirby grabbed a box of matches from the utility drawer and unlocked the back door.

"Howdy, neighbor. Did you two beautiful ladies have a good day?"

If she stood on her tiptoes she could see over the top of the fence. There he was, standing on his back deck, where a new gas grill gleamed in the warm sunshine. "All in all, no complaints. How about you two handsome guys?"

"Me and Leo had an excellent time. We flew up to the Blackfeet Reservation. There was a museum there I wanted to take a look at. Really enjoyed it."

"Leo went with you?"

"Not in the museum, no, but he did love the ride."

"In the helicopter?"

"Sure. He's been up in the air with me since he was nine weeks old. He loves to fly. Unlike some people. Yeah, I noticed your white knuckles on our flight back from Seattle that day."

"It was the storm."

"Well, you should have said something. I would have told you how I've flown in dust storms, ice storms, blizzards, lightning, thunder, under heavy fire, through the middle of an enemy tank division and about in every other condition known to man. I've only crashed twice."

"*Twice?* That's not going to make me feel better."

"Hey, I lived to tell about it. I'm a first-class crash pilot. They train you for that kind of thing, you know. They don't give you a chopper worth millions just to wreck it." He winked, trying to make light of it.

She saw the grief in his eyes. Hard times, Ruth had said. Well, Kirby knew it wasn't any of her business, but she was curious. She couldn't help it.

"Aren't you supposed to be starting a new job or something? What did I hear?" Sam lifted the grill's lid. "Oh, I see that grin. It was today, wasn't it? How'd it go?"

"Great. It's a lot of responsibility, but I'll love it." How did she tell him about it? About having her own clinic, with staff to run, decisions to make, patients to see, illnesses to diagnose? "I even got to put in five stitches."

"Five whole stitches?"

"A little boy put his hand through a glass door. I stitched up his little palm very carefully, and he shouldn't have much of a scar. He'll be as good as new in a few weeks."

"Let me guess. You give out lollipops, don't you?"

"I do, and—wait, stop laughing at me. It's not funny." Sam could imagine just how she'd comforted that little boy. He couldn't help feeling a little envious.

Everybody needed comfort now and then.

Well, except tough guys like him. "What do you think you're doing?"

"Lighting my barbecue."

That did it. His first night of barbecuing on his own back deck of his own house, something he'd wanted for a heck of a long time, and it wasn't right, that's what, to see her over there looking a little lonely on this big night. She was happy about her new job and wanting to celebrate her big day, and she was alone on her deck with her dog.

Neither of them had someone.

"Hold on a minute, will you?" He left his long-handled grill spatula on the deck rail beside the plate with the one hamburger patty he had thawed. He had a whole stack of them frozen solid in his freezer. He didn't have a microwave yet—he was going to wait until his kitchen remodel was done—and that was a problem. "So, what were you going to cook on your grill?"

"A hamburger."

"You got it thawed and ready to go?"

"Well, I have the hamburger package in my refrigerator. Did you need to borrow some? I'd be happy to—"

"No, Miss Good Samaritan." Sam shook his head. Could she be any nicer? "Toss that package over here, and I'll grill up your burger. It's the least I can do, considering it's your first day and you've been such a good neighbor. I really appreciate it when you have those sisters of yours over that you keep the drum playing and rock music down to a low rumble."

"Are you saying you want to have supper together?"

"I could suffer through it. Can Leo come, too?"

"Leo is always welcome."

Hearing his name, the dog looked up from his huge hunk of rawhide and barked.

"Looks like you've got a deal. Toss me the hamburger and I'll get cookin'."

"Toss it to you?"

"Sure. I know how to catch."

The way he grinned made her heart leap. She knew this wasn't a date—it wasn't that kind of invitation. This was just two neighbors, two people alone, having supper together. She wasn't going to start letting herself hope that this could be anything more than that.

While Jessie raced around the backyard stretching her legs, Kirby found the package of hamburger meat on the bottom shelf of the refrigerator and carried it out to the deck rail. She flung it.

Sam snatched the package out of the air like a major league shortstop. "You like your burger rare? Medium rare?"

"Well done, but not charred."

"As the lady likes." Sam saluted her.

Suddenly there was so much to do. She had to change out of her work clothes. Preheat the oven. Empty the dishwasher. Put the fries on to bake. Oh, make a salad for two. Happier than she'd felt in years, she scurried about, preparing for Sam's invasion.

She took the trash out, but Sam wasn't on his deck. The burgers were sizzling away and smelled delicious. As she raced Jessie to the gate, she heard Leo bark on the other side of the fence.

Her feet felt light and it was easy to unlatch the gate and keep running, the dog at her heels. They skidded to a stop at the back of the carport, where she tossed the small bag into the garbage can. Then she raced her dog back to the deck.

"I'm coming over in a few," Sam called as he emerged from his back door, spatula and platter in hand. "Be prepared."

"Is that supposed to scare me?"

"Sure. Leo and I are entering enemy territory. Women territory. I saw all those ruffled curtains and the lace tablecloth. I think I can survive it."

"You're a brave man, Sam Gardner."

So she was laughing as she slipped out of her drab work clothes and into her favorite pair of jeans and a cheerful long-sleeved T-shirt, one with a row of daisies imprinted on the front, smiling up at the sun. That's how she felt.

Happy. *Not* hopeful.

When he walked into her house, he looked rugged in his faded army T-shirt and paint-streaked denims. Leo didn't look right or left, but loped straight through the living room to the kitchen. Jessie came running in from the backyard, delighted to see her new friend. The two sniffed noses, then ran off together in search of the dog biscuit box.

"Done to perfection," he said of the steaming beef patties on the platter he held. He clutched two bottles in his other hand. "Steak and barbecue sauces. I didn't know what you liked, so I brought both."

"That's great. I've got cheese slices and fresh buns. It'll take me just a second to slice tomatoes and onions—"

The thud of something heavy hitting the linoleum was followed by the skid and scatter of dog biscuits tumbling across the floor.

"Leo! That's no way to behave in a lady's house." Sam shook his head. "That boy has no manners. Leo, you're about as suave as I am. Sit. I mean it."

The rambunctious dog wasn't intimidated, and the warmth in Sam's voice said that he was always kind, even when he was correcting the dog's behavior.

Sam shoved the bottles and the platter of meat onto the edge of the island and knelt to both dogs. "Hey, Jess. What a good girl you are, eating only one. Unlike my Leo. Scarfing as many biscuits as you can. That's uncouth, boy. It's no way to impress the ladies."

Sam ran one big hand over his dog's broad head. When Jessie waggled, begging politely for the same, Sam laid his other hand on her round head, stroking gently, and the spaniel sighed with happiness.

Kind to animals. Wasn't that on her Mr. Perfect list?

Kirby's knees went weak. Her heart stood still and peace filled her, reaching her soul.

A peace that felt like sunlight touching the earth for the first time, chasing away all the dark places with the promise of the first spring.

It took all her strength of character to sit down at the table as though nothing had happened. As though she hadn't fallen in love with Sam Gardner.

A man who didn't love her.

The stars winked, bright and perfect, in a foreign sky. Not the constellations Sam had grown up with. No moon to help him out, either. Deep in enemy territory, with a squad of tired SEALs waiting for him in the jungle, his navigator—his best friend—unconscious and in shock and his copilot bleeding to death.

He felt ancient, as if he'd lived too long, seen too much, been here before. He had enough medical training to wrap the wounds and stabilize Mark's broken femur. Needing to stabilize Chris's neck, he dragged a board from the back of the smoking chopper.

Pain galvanized him. He worked, and worked fast, knowing he didn't have much time to find cover for his men. He hoped the PJs coming to get him would be here but quick.

Pain wasn't the only thing that motivated

him. His wedding ring burned like a reminder of all that was important in his life—

Sam woke up, sweat rolling down his face.

Dreaming again. The memories stayed with him as he made his way to the kitchen. The past felt close tonight, closer than it had been in a long while.

He grabbed a soda from the fridge and saw a flash of muted light in the window of the house next door. Kirby's house. Judging from the faint glow in the living room window, she had the television on. At 1:43 a.m. He didn't believe his eyes.

Miss Good Samaritan had trouble sleeping, did she?

Well, she wasn't alone on that score. He stood sucking down the cold cola and debated for a good twenty minutes. There were a thousand reasons he shouldn't go knock on her door.

The late hour. It was inappropriate to visit her in his pajamas. She'd probably think he was a burglar sneaking around in her yard. It would probably look as if he cared about her in a special way.

There was only one reason that mattered. He wanted to make sure she was all right.

He pulled on a pair of sweats, left Leo sound asleep in the bedroom and made one stop in the kitchen before grabbing his keys and locking the back door behind him.

Leaves waved in the pleasant night air as he marched down the walk, hopped over the fence and circled around the side of her house. No lights were on, just the TV. He stomped up the front steps, taking care to make some noise so he wouldn't startle her. He raised his hand to knock.

The door swung open to reveal Kirby in the faint light cast by the TV screen. With her hair tied back in a ponytail and wearing an oversize blue fluffy sleeper with feet, she looked to be about the cutest thing he'd ever seen.

"You nearly scared me to death, Sam Gardner."

Cute, but mad. He held out his peace offering. "I saw your TV on and I got worried. Am I pardoned?"

"All right, but only because you brought chocolate ice cream."

"Not just chocolate. The kind with fudge swirls and marshmallows."

"Now I'll invite you in, as long as you promise to be on your best behavior."

"Sweetheart, I can't promise you that." He stalked past her, shut the door.

He looked athletic and fit and wonderfully masculine with his tousled hair and unshaven jaw.

What did she look like at two in the morning? Disaster. Her hair had been pulled back without benefit of a mirror. Since she'd washed her face before bedtime, she had no cover-up on to disguise the freckles on her nose and what was the start of a blemish on her forehead above her right brow. It had only been a small smudge earlier, but it probably looked like a bull's eye by now.

She'd pulled the one-piece sleeper on over her nightshirt because it was cozy and comfy. But the bulky fleece made her look at least twenty pounds heavier than usual. See what a good thing it was that Sam wasn't interested in her?

Because if he was, and he saw her like this, he'd change his mind.

By the time she'd caught up with him, he'd taken command of her kitchen. He had located the ice cream scoop and already had the lid off the ice cream carton. "What are we watching?"

"An Alfred Hitchcock thriller is on the

classic movie channel." Kirby stole two clean cereal bowls from the top rack of her dishwasher.

"I love Hitchcock." Sam began scooping huge hunks of rich chocolate ice cream into both bowls.

"Why were you awake to see that my TV was on?" she asked, grabbing spoons out of the drawer.

"I couldn't sleep." He secured the lid on the carton and tucked it into the freezer for safekeeping. He turned around, spotted the spaniel waddling down the hall and into the dimly lit kitchen.

"Look who woke up." Sam knelt and held out his hand in greeting. "Hi, Jess. Are you going to let me stay and watch a movie with you two beautiful girls?"

Did Sam Gardner have to be so perfect? "Jess, be careful of this man. He thinks he can flatter us so we won't mind his brash and uncivilized behavior, barging into our house at this time of night. Compromising our reputations."

"Everybody has a gift, and that's mine."

"Oh, so you think you can just help yourself to whatever is in my fridge?"

"We men who tarnish reputations take what we want. Isn't that right, Jess?"

The dog sighed happily, surrendering the underside of her chin for Sam's gentle fingertips.

See? Even her dog thought he was perfect.

"Fetch me the milk, would you?" Sam asked as he switched from chin to ear and made the spaniel sigh with appreciation.

"First you invite yourself into my house and then you start bossing me around."

"I take orders, too, but I don't see you giving any."

She grabbed the milk, but while she was trying to think of a snappy comeback, he'd already commandeered one of her saucepans and was turning on the controls to the stove.

She pushed him out of the way with her hip. "Give me that. I can't believe you know what you're doing."

It was like trying to move a mountain, but he gave a little, so she could at least reach the temperature knobs. She adjusted the heat, took the carton back and poured the right amount for two into the pan.

"I usually rely on chamomile tea, but warmed milk sounds good tonight." She wasn't going to let him know she'd been thinking about making some cocoa.

"Cocoa should never be savored alone. It gains something with good company." Sam dug the tin out of his grocery sack. "My own homemade mix. Actually, a military buddy of mine got the recipe from his grandmother. Sweet chocolate, sugar and more powdered chocolate. Trust me. This will heal what troubles you."

"Oh, it's miracle cocoa, is it?"

"Yep. The secret ingredients are the mini-marshmallows. Give me your two biggest mugs. Wait, don't tell me you only have those dainty china ones with flowers on them and those itty-bitty handles?"

"That's the kind of thing you register for a wedding. Notice I'm not married?" Kirby opened the cabinets.

"Nothing is stopping you from buying cups and plates. Unless you're upset about the not being married thing."

Embarrassed, she snatched the popcorn packets from him, yanked open the microwave door and didn't answer.

"Why should you feel bad about not being married? I see a woman who hasn't settled. Wait until you find true love, that's my advice, because marriage is forever. Trust me. That ceremony is more than a dress and getting the engraved napkins just right. It's a tie that will forever bind you, and it's best not done in haste or for the wrong reasons."

"You're being serious, huh?"

"I can be."

"It becomes you. Do it more often."

"Now who's bossy?"

"Me, and I like it. Get the mugs, would you?"

While the milk warmed, Sam stirred in the miracle cocoa mix in slow sprinkles, his head bent to the task, his dark shock of hair falling forward to hide his face.

Wait until you find true love, he'd said. It sounded as though he knew what he was talking about.

Had his wife been that for him, his true love? "Thanks for your advice. Are you glad you didn't settle?"

"Oh, I settled." He didn't look at her as he snatched one of the mugs out of her hand. Then the other.

The grief was back, the sadness.

"Why can't you sleep?" he asked as he poured the steaming milk. "There isn't a rock band next door rehearsing."

"I am blessed to have you for my neighbor. You're wonderfully quiet at night."

"You're not answering my question."

"I'm too worked up about my new job, maybe. And feeling alone." Because it was too honest, she grabbed the ice cream bowls and took off so she could pretend she hadn't been. She was grateful for the dim light from the television so she wouldn't have to look him in the eye.

She set the bowls of ice cream on the coffee table. She'd forgotten the spoons.

He set the steaming mugs on the table next to the ice cream. The rich scent of chocolate rose on the air as Kirby spun on her heels and headed back to the kitchen.

She was letting herself be too affected. He'd come as a neighbor, as a friend. She rescued the popcorn from the microwave and filled her favorite bowl with the fluffy kernels.

He wasn't holding on to a secret affection for her. She needed to remember to take his friendship at face value.

"What's taking so long in there? Did you stop for a quick game of Monopoly?"

"*What* did you say?" She grabbed the spoons from the counter. "Were you *spying* on me?"

"In some circles it's called reconnaissance, and that's not a bad thing."

"You *were* spying on me. Shame on you."

"Hey, you were the one who left your blinds up after dark. How is it my fault that when I went outside to lock up, the light from your kitchen window glowed like a beacon in the dark and made me look?"

"Made you look? You were helpless to look away, huh?"

"Sure was. I can't remember the last time I saw so many pretty women playing a board game."

"You think I'm boring."

"That's not what I meant. I just couldn't believe my eyes."

He was laughing at her! She marched around the corner of the couch, set the spoons on the table in front of them and *refused* to look at him. "It's not funny. People play board games all the time."

"I know."

"My sisters and I like to play. We always have."

"Yes, and eat ice cream sundaes while you do."

"That was dessert."

"Hey, I believe you." Sam helped himself to her remote and turned up the volume.

Kirby's dog padded in, eyes droopy with sleep, and circled three times at the foot of the couch.

Maybe it was her turn to interrogate him. "You never answered me. Why can't you sleep?"

"Oh, I tried, but the trouble with sleeping is the dreaming." He dug his spoon into the melty ice cream. "It's called post-traumatic stress. It's pretty common for the soldiers who've seen combat. Sometimes it's worse than others."

"And tonight?"

"I dreamed about when I was captured behind enemy lines." He set the spoon down with a rattle against the bowl.

Kirby noticed his hands were shaking. "That had to be horrible."

"It was. I was trained well for it, but it was horrible." His face turned into granite.

Kirby didn't know what to say. She'd wondered what hardships Sam Gardner had endured. Now she knew. Her heart ached for him.

"Hitchcock is great." Sam leaned back into the cushions.

He seemed as if he'd rather not talk about it anymore, so she didn't press him. But she watched him—so big and strong, and stronger now that she knew his hardships. His pain.

Life had a way of marking everyone.

She willed away her own sadness about the plane accident that often troubled her so she couldn't sleep. It had been the day she'd broken in two, never to be the same again.

They ate ice cream in silence and drank the best cocoa she'd ever tasted. While the movie played, she snuggled up in the corner of the couch and watched. Now and then over handfuls of popcorn she'd sneak glances at Sam, who appeared to be engrossed in the story.

Just the way he stirred her soul when he reached across the cushions and his hand settled over hers proved he was the right man.

Chapter Nine

"Earth to Kirby." Humor sparkled in Monica's voice as she set the stack of folders on the counter. "Come back to earth, girl. There's a kid in exam room four waiting for you."

"A kid?" Kirby blinked, remembering where she was. Standing in the hallway closest to the waiting room that echoed with the sounds of coughing and sneezing children. "A patient. Oh, right."

"I can't believe you. Whatever you were thinking about, you were totally absorbed." The nurse winked. "Or is it who? A handsome suitor, maybe? Mr. Right?"

Her face flamed. Heat scorched all the way to her hairline.

"That's what I thought." Monica left the

clipboard on the counter and padded off down the hallway. "Someone's in love."

Yes, but I don't admit it. This was the third time today she'd been thinking of Sam so hard that she'd forgotten where she was and what she was doing.

When she ought to be charting, her mind drifted back to last night. Snuggled on the couch, with the TV's soft light filtering over her, with Sam at her side. Not close enough to cuddle together, but close. She loved the way he would turn to her and comment on the movie in a low, vibrating baritone that was intimate and wonderful and warm all at once.

Every time she thought of him, she felt that way. Warm, the way she did with the spring sunshine on her face. Happy, as if her problems were melting away. Enlivened, as if the May weather outside was blooming in her heart.

She couldn't wait to see him again.

She glanced down at the chart. The last name was Bemis. Not Janice from high school—the one who always called her by her sister's name. Kirby wanted to groan, but, hey, she could handle it. She could handle that woman.

She opened the door and put a smile on her face.

"Hello, Janice."

"Kendra. I've been calling you, but you haven't returned my messages. I'm desperate." Janice shifted her baby to her other arm so her hand was free to pat at her hair. "We've got two more months until the reunion, and I need volunteers!"

"You haven't left any messages on my answering machine."

"But—"

"Maybe you aren't calling the right sister. I'm Kirby, not Kendra, and I'm not interested in volunteering with you." That done as politely as she could manage it, Kirby turned her attention to the little boy who sat on the exam table, swinging his legs.

At first glance she noticed he was flushed, and the temperature noted on his chart confirmed that. "Hi there, Christopher. You didn't go to school today, huh?"

"Nope, 'cause I keep coughing up real yucky stuff."

"That's a good reason not to go to school." Kirby grabbed a wooden tongue blade. "This won't hurt a bit. Can you open wide and say 'aah'? That's right. Good job."

She tossed the blade into the waste container and pulled her otoscope out of her pocket. "Do your ears hurt?"

"Nah, but they feel funny."

"I'd better take a look there, too." Kirby glanced into both ear canals. The tympanic membranes were red. Nothing serious, though.

"Oh, my. Well, I thought…" Janice looked perplexed. "Maybe I can still beg you to help me. There's so much left to do—"

"No." She'd never said that word without feeling guilty before, but she did it. "I've got my hands full with my new job and my family."

"Oh." Janice's polite smile faded.

Turning back to the little boy, Kirby went to her stethoscope. "This isn't going to hurt, I promise. I just want to listen to your lungs. Can you breathe in really slowly and out really slowly? Through your mouth. That's right."

Kirby heard what she expected. Coarse and junky—yep, it was what she'd been hearing all morning from children and adults alike. Christopher had it, too.

"It looks like you are pretty sick. You've got bronchitis, so you get to stay home from school for the rest of the week."

"Do I gotta get a shot?" Christopher eyed her warily, ready to put up a struggle.

"Nope. It's your lucky day. Janice, he needs rest and lots of fluids. I'll give you a prescription for some really great cough syrup, which will make him more comfortable."

"Thank you." The words came clipped, and the harsh fluorescent light overhead illuminated the dark circles beneath her eyes that her carefully applied makeup could not hide.

Kirby knew a mother's job wasn't an easy one. "How's the baby been? Is she sounding wheezy? Is she having trouble eating?"

"No, she's just been extra fussy."

"Keep an eye on her temperature. Give me a call if you think she's catching this. I'm going to send in a prescription for antibiotics for Christopher. You use the drugstore uptown, don't you? They'll have the order ready when you get there."

"That will save me some time. Thanks, Kirby."

"You're welcome." No one's life was as perfect as it looked, Kirby knew. Everyone could use help now and then. "What about you? Want me to take a look while you're here?"

"I have been coughing, but that's all. I'm

sure I can fight it off. I have to. I don't have time to get sick."

"Then I'll give you the same orders. Get as much rest as you can. Plenty of fluids. The cough medicine will work for you, too. Give me a call if that changes." Kirby opened the top cabinet over the sink and held out a canister of Tootsie Pops. "Christopher, you did a great job. Are you going to go home and help take care of your mom and sister?"

He chose a purple sucker. "Yep. *I'm* the big brother."

"You're a fantastic one, too." Kirby put away the canister and opened the door. "Take care, Janice."

"You, too, Kirby."

Well, that was one problem solved. Kirby updated Christopher's chart as she headed across the hall to the nearest computer. Email was a wonderful invention, she mused as she zipped off an electronic prescription to the local pharmacy.

Noise from the waiting room drifted down the corridor. By the sounds of it, she was going to have another long day. She'd been hoping to get off work on time, because wouldn't it be nice to see Sam on his deck again, getting ready to barbecue?

Sam. Her entire being sighed. She loved the welcoming grin that had lit him up when he'd spotted her last night over the fence. And later, when they'd eaten dinner and talked about their dogs, his solid, masculine presence had dwarfed her small eating nook. How companionable it had been sharing a meal and conversation with him.

Would he be waiting for her tonight? Or, maybe, should she be the one to cook? To invite him over?

"You look so happy, I hate to bother you." Monica rapped on the open door as she sashayed in. She laid a pile of folders on the desk next to the computer. "There's a call for you. Line five."

"Thanks." She grabbed the receiver.

Maybe if she were really efficient the rest of the afternoon, she wouldn't get out of here *too* late. Maybe she'd stop by the video rental store on the way home and grab an old movie.

"Kirby? It's Jeremiah." The doctor wasn't only a volunteer, but worked at the free clinic. "It's great you have your own practice. I know how hard you worked for that. I hope my job recommendation helped."

"It did, thank you. What can I do for you?"

"I heard back on little Sarah. She's home and doing better. She's still on a waiting list for a donor match, and we're hopeful. I'm getting a team together for when we get the call. Are you in?"

"Absolutely."

"That's what I wanted to hear. I'll be in touch."

Kirby hung up the phone. Her first thought was of Sam. Because he'd probably be flying them when the time came, she thought, but it was just a rationalization.

She thought of him not because he was their pilot. She thought of him because she loved him.

Did he love her? Only time would tell. But last night had given her hope.

See how her thoughts kept circling around to him?

Stop thinking about him. But there she was, thinking of Sam *again*.

The rest of the afternoon would seem like an eternity until she could be with him.

An eternity had passed and with it her optimism. It was seven o'clock before she locked the clinic's back door behind her. The sun was heading swiftly for the mountain-rimmed horizon. Well past the dinner hour.

Disappointment felt like a heavy stone in her chest. Okay, so the day hadn't turned out as she'd expected. She'd stayed to treat every last patient. That had resulted in a ton of paperwork. If Sam had been watching for her and waiting to cook supper, then he'd have given up by now.

There was no sense in stopping by the video store or hurrying home now.

The sun was setting, and a chill was creeping into the air, for there was still snow on the nearby mountains. *Maybe* she could still see him, she reasoned as she hit the remote and opened her car door.

When she went home, she would let Jessie out. And if she *happened* to accompany her dog into the backyard, then there was a chance Sam would be in his yard with his dog. They could at least chat over the fence. She could find out where he and Leo had flown off to today.

Maybe, when she got home, she'd flip through the television guide to see if there was a good movie on. Then she could invite him over, pop corn and sit together on the couch. Didn't that sound like a good plan?

Her stomach grumbled fiercely as she backed out of the parking spot and into the alley. First she'd hunt down some food. She took the back street through town and caught sight of the lit neon sign of the local drive-in. The perfect solution.

What if Sam wasn't outside when she took Jessie out? What if there wasn't a good movie on TV? These were definite problems in her plan.

What was she doing plotting and planning anyway? She ought to be ashamed of herself. If Sam were to be her one true love, then they would wind up together. No amount of planning on her part would influence the outcome. But if she happened to run into Sam, she would ask him over to watch a movie.

The local drive-in was an old cinder-block building neatly painted in a tidy white with dark blue trim. She pulled up to the microphone and studied her options. The white eraser board tacked up next to the hand-painted menu sign touted the daily specials.

"Hey, is that you, Kirby?" Misty Collins asked over the speaker.

"How did you know it was me?" Misty was her sister Karen's good friend. "Wait, I know, you saw my car drive past the side window."

"Guilty. Hey, are you going to go for the usual?"

"Absolutely." Kirby pulled around to the drive-through window and handed over a five-dollar bill.

"How's the new job working out?" Misty turned to pull change from her till.

"Great." She could look right past Misty into the restaurant.

There, behind the counter, was a curve of muscled shoulder. Wait, she knew that shoulder. Her gaze traveled up the column of his neck to the square jaw.

Sam. As if he felt her presence, he pivoted, his gaze riveting on her like a bullet finding its target. Leaving her pinned. Overwhelmed. Amazed.

Awareness jolted through her like an electric current. An emotional awareness of high voltage that zinged from her heart to her soul.

Trembling from the shock, Kirby realized Misty was waiting for her. She held out her hand, accepted the change. She dropped the quarters and nickels and pennies into her purse, unable to break away.

The world around her vanished. The lavender glare of twilight, the rush of the wind from the air conditioner, the clang of the old cash register as Misty slammed the drawer shut.

There was only Sam. He filled her vision.

Then the hard line of his mouth softened into a crooked grin. One dark brow arched in a question.

A question she felt deep in her heart. A question she heard as clearly as if he'd spoken. Want to come in and join me?

Yes, she answered with all the power of her being.

His grin broadened and became a smile that was an answer, an answer that blazed in his dark eyes.

It was the look of a man interested. Sam Gardner was interested in her.

"Here's your burger." Unaware, Misty handed the bag of food and the heavy cup through the window and broke the moment. She moved fully into the window and blocked Kirby's view of Sam. "Have a good evening."

"Th-thanks." Shaken, Kirby set the bag on the passenger floor and the cold milk shake in the cup holder. Her hands were cold and trembling. She felt as if her spine had turned to Jell-O. Somehow she put her car in gear and pulled forward.

The wide lit windows of the drive-in glowed in invitation as she pulled into a parking spot in the front.

There was Sam, standing in the window, shrugging out of his leather bomber jacket, revealing the T-shirt beneath. An old, olive-green T-shirt that said U.S. Army in faded, wash-worn script.

He tossed the jacket onto the booth's seat. Everything he did, every movement he made was powerful, masculine, sure.

He made every other man in existence seem ordinary. As if he could make gravity stop working and the world stop spinning. At least, that's the way it *seemed* as she floated from her car to the restaurant.

He was already watching her, standing like a gentleman, and he waited as she slipped into the red cushioned bench across from him. He sat after she did.

"What's a good girl like you doing in a place like this? I would have pegged you for a wholesome, home-cooking sort." He eyed the supersized foam cup she lowered to the table.

"I had to work late, and I was too tired

and hungry to even think of going home and cooking. Besides, a bacon cheeseburger *is* wholesome. At least in my book."

"A bacon double-cheeseburger." Grinning, he held up his sandwich, thick and dripping with grease and everything good. "I had a late day, too. Got wrapped up with an inspection and paperwork, and the fire department nailed me because I didn't have a working fire extinguisher in my office. Everything else was good, and considering I just took over the place, I think they could have been more lenient."

"I don't know. You look like a rule breaker to me. The sort that if you give an inch, you'll take a mile."

"Nope, I'm one of the good guys. The fire chief could have been more understanding. I was so wrapped up in paperwork that I didn't get to go up today."

"You mean fly?"

He nodded, grabbed three fries and dragged them through the tiny paper cup brimming with tartar sauce. "I fly every day. It gives me some peace to be up away from everything. It gives me perspective."

"What perspective is that?"

"Don't sweat the small stuff. We're lucky

to be here, alive on this earth, with all that comes with it." He took a big hungry bite of his burger.

"That's how I feel in my garden. All the world and its strife and my problems big and small fade away when I'm working with my roses." Kirby reached into her white paper sack and withdrew a large packet of golden fries and a plastic container of tartar.

"I noticed all those prickly bushes along the fence line. I think I broke a few branches when I repaired the fence." He felt bad now, although he'd been careful at the time. "Did you plant all those yourself?"

"Not all of them. The rose garden was the reason I bought the house. Even though it was more than I wanted to pay."

"Ah, now the truth comes out. You've got yourself a mortgage payment you can't quite afford."

"Hey, I resent the way you said that. You make me sound like one of those stereotypical women who can't manage their money." Kirby unfolded a paper napkin and set her fries and container of tartar on it, neat as a pin.

"How true is it?" He was proud of the way his voice sounded light, as if he were teasing her, but a hard cold stone had settled in his gut. A bad feeling that felt way too familiar.

That was the reason Carla had married him, she'd told him. After he'd spent twenty-three days as a prisoner of war.

"Okay, so I had to put extra money down so I could just squeak into qualifying for the mortgage, but I did it. And my savings suffered for it, especially when I didn't get the promotion at the hospital I'd put in for. I finished my master's this last December and I thought I'd get a better job right away, but—" She shrugged.

No, Kirby was nothing like Carla, marrying for financial advantage. What was he doing confusing the two? He was hungrier than he thought, so he unwrapped his second bacon double cheeseburger. "You wanted a job in management?"

"Oh, no. I loved patient care, but I wanted to do more. That's why I wanted to become a nurse-practitioner."

Wanted to do more? She was a real Mary Poppins, wasn't she? She lit up like a dawn sky, genuine and lovely. He didn't doubt her sincerity. She shone down to her soul.

She unwrapped her hamburger with careful

precision. "Having my own clinic and helping people is all I've ever wanted to do."

See? She was nothing like Carla, and this was what all his turmoil had been about. The return of the dreams, the memories of the crash. It was Kirby's doing. She made him wish his poor battered heart could love again.

What man wouldn't wish for a woman like her? Look at her. She talked on about her day at work and all the people she'd helped. She wanted to make a difference—at least, she tried to, she said. She lifted one delicate shoulder in an uncertain shrug.

"I know you make a difference." He remembered the competent and caring nurse she'd been on board the flight to Seattle. A volunteer's flight. She volunteered when she was on a tight budget.

Didn't that say everything about her? Everything he would ever need to know? She wasn't the kind of woman who had ulterior motives or the type who was always looking for the easiest path. No, she'd worked hard, put herself through school and was independent. She managed her money, had her own house and a career she worked hard at.

There was a lot to respect about her. A lot to trust in her.

The more time he spent with Kirby, the more he found to admire in her.

And the more flawed he felt.

What was he doing here, anyway? He'd meant to grab food and take it home to Leo. That's what he should be doing.

But why? He'd go home to a house that echoed around him. And spend his evening working on dismantling the kitchen cabinets. No, he was content right here.

The door opened with a gust of wind and a ring of children's voices. Two little boys pushed playfully at each other, arguing over who would hold the door for their mom, who carried a big purse and a bulging diaper bag over one shoulder. She was followed by her husband, cradling a pink-swathed infant in his arms.

Kirby glanced over her shoulder, and the longing on her face was as obvious as the tile floor at their feet.

"You're looking to get married," he stated flat out, not believing he'd actually come right out and said it.

And why not? He might as well make it clear. If they were going to share suppers and watch movies, then it would be as friends. And only friends.

"Yes, but I told you. I'm waiting for my one true love." Her eyes turned dreamy as she watched the family crowd close to the counter, the little boys talking over each other trying to be the first to order.

"You're getting close to thirty. You're not tempted to grab the first guy who comes along?"

"Where is this coming from? *You're* the one who advised me never to settle."

He took a big bite, finished his burger and chewed. Conveniently, it was too impolite to answer with his mouth full.

She scowled at him, in the nice way she had. "I know. You men think you're not safe from a woman who'd like to get married. But you're wrong. A good marriage and the blessing of children would be the most wonderful gift. But it's the love that gives life its meaning."

Maybe that's why he felt so aimless. Restless. Sam crumpled the empty burger wrapping and tossed it onto his tray. This was all too philosophical for him. "I'm waiting for my one true love, too."

"Now you're teasing me." She tossed a French fry at him.

He snatched it out of the air before it could bonk him in the forehead. "Hey! Be careful. If you want war, I know how to fight."

"So do I." She lobbed a little overcooked French fry missile at him.

He punched it and it skidded across the table. "See? You're outgunned. Are you willing to surrender?"

"Not unless you're offering acceptable terms."

"Me? Why should I? You're the one needing to surrender." To prove his point, he blasted two rapid-fire fries her way. They bounced harmlessly off her milk-shake container. "Warning shots," he explained, gathering more ammo. "Surrender, agree to being taken my prisoner and I'll be kind."

Kirby took up another fry, trouble twinkling in her eyes as she considered. "Prisoner? That doesn't sound like a favorable condition for me."

"Maybe. Maybe not. It's a risk you'll have to take. Either way, it's a shame to waste these fries. They're made from real potatoes. Mmm, good."

She laughed and made him laugh, too. She

made him feel way too much, and he didn't like it.

Not at all. He was a big, tough loner of a man who didn't need anyone.

The family that had come in had finished ordering and broke away from the counter like a football team from a huddle. The little boys dashed full speed through the restaurant, eager and shoving. Both parents told them to slow down.

He couldn't stand to look at the happy family. The kind he could never have because he was never going to get married again. How could he? His heart was gone and he couldn't get it back.

Ever.

At least Kirby seemed to understand that. And he appreciated her for it.

"Are you done? C'mon, let's take our milk shakes and get out of here."

"I didn't agree to being your prisoner." She was all that was good in the world, and he knew it.

He'd found what he hadn't believed existed. A good woman with a loving heart. There wasn't a selfish, hurtful bone in her.

He was crazy and he couldn't explain it, but the thought of being away from her hurt as badly as a bullet through the middle of his chest.

He'd keep her with him for as long as he could.

Then he'd have to say goodbye.

He held out his hand. "Come with me. There's something I want to show you."

Chapter Ten

"**W**hat do you think?" He held the chopper steady, so she could watch the dark bowl of night chase the last of the twilight across the sky.

"This is fantastic. I wouldn't m-miss this for the world."

Was that a tremble he heard?

He hazarded a look through the shadowed cockpit. It looked to him as if she was gripping the edge of her seat pretty hard. "You're scared?"

"How could you guess?"

"Relax. I know what I'm doing. This is supposed to be fun, right? To get away from it all."

"Y-yes. Sure. Does this qualify as cruel and unusual punishment?"

Now she told him she didn't want to go flying? "Have a little faith in me, Kirby. I'm not such a bad guy."

"I know."

He had the sudden urge to show off a little, to show her what he could do, but she was pretty white-knuckled. She'd been that way on the trip back from Seattle, he remembered.

He banked—not too tight, just enough to nose them around to face the white-capped mountains ringing the eastern horizon. Man, they were something. Big, rugged, bold. Close enough to touch. "Open your eyes, Kirby."

"I don't like sitting up front. I feel like I'm going to fall straight to the ground."

"I won't let that happen. I promise. Enjoy the view. Have some fun."

"This *is* fun. I've had so much I'm ready to go home."

"Not yet. Wait. Watch for it...." He nodded toward the horizon, where darkness crept over the rim of the mountains. "Right there. Keep looking right over the white caps. Don't blink or you'll miss it. And *relax*. I hardly ever crash. Really."

"That makes me feel so much better," she quipped and resisted the urge to roll her eyes.

Was he laughing at her?

Kirby wanted to look at him, but it was hard considering she was frozen stiff in fear and turning her head was a major effort. In the shadows, with the faint green glow from the panels, he looked like a pirate at sea, bold and powerful, a sheer renegade.

Have faith in him? No way—he was enjoying this a little too much.

"You really don't like to fly?" How could he say that and sound so innocent? He had to have figured it out by now.

"No."

"But you volunteer for medical flights."

"Yes, but I don't like it." She was thankful Sam was at least keeping the helicopter level. "I'm in the back and I'm busy, so I can pretend I'm not up in the sky dangling way too high above the ground."

"I didn't know. Well, don't worry. Stick with me and I'll show you there's a lot to like about flying."

He had to be a good pilot. He looked calm, in control, able to handle any situation. Really, she trusted him. But accidents happened. "You mentioned you've crashed before…?"

"Look." Instead of answering her, he pointed to the eastern horizon.

The first star of the night peeked out of the haze of twilight, flickering like a newly lit flame, sputtering and then shining strong and bright and true.

"It's breathtaking."

"Quick, make a wish."

His gaze locked on her as tangible and as reverent as a tender touch to the side of her face.

She shivered deep inside, where she was vulnerable. Where she felt her heart opening to him against her will.

She was in love with him. Way too in love with him for her own good.

Did she dare to hope that he could love her in return? Was it possible?

His hand covered hers, where she gripped the seat so tightly. He peeled her fingers from the curve of the cushion and took her hand in his. A startling, electric shock zinged up her arm and ended in her soul.

It was like the star burning to life through the darkness, a bright diamond glow where only darkness had been before, and now was a blazing light that would burn for millions of years.

She felt bright with it, consumed with the growing love inside her.

"You saw the star first," she whispered. "You make the wish."

"I wish for your wish. For whatever your heart desires." His big fingers squeezed hers with care. "Go ahead and dream a little."

Her heart already knew the answer. She didn't have to form the thought in her mind or utter a word. Life had been endlessly good to her. She had good health, a good family, wonderful sisters she could count on. Her job, her house, her dog, her friends, her happiness.

But she wanted the sweetest gift of all. True love.

Please, is it too much to ask?

"Wish made?" Sam's fingers squeezed hers again, holding on.

She never wanted him to let go. But when she nodded, he moved away as if their closeness had never been.

In the broad sweep of sky, stars appeared like magic, one after another as the twilight became night. Shimmering carat gems, brilliant white against the deepening black.

Awe filled her. She worked so hard and was so busy, always coming and going, she hadn't taken time to look at the beauty around her. To appreciate the sweetness of living, simply of being alive.

"There, you finally relaxed."

Sam's words, the beat of the blades overhead and the vibration of the engine through the metal frame reminded her of where she was. Dangling up in the sky, where only stars and eagles belonged.

The sound was what she remembered first. The horrible crash of thunder the same moment lightning burned her eyes, the boom of metal, the roar of the engine as it blew. And then absolute silence, so loud it vibrated in her ears as the private plane fell to earth.

They'd crashed in the Bridger Mountains, the same ones she was looking at.

Fear exploded inside her. She clamped her mouth shut, squeezed her eyes shut and clutched the seat that was steady and level. See? She was safe. Perfectly safe. The mild vibration from the engine and the *whomp, whomp, whomp* of the blades were proof of that.

"Hey, what's wrong?"

"I'm fine." She couldn't tell him, this rogue pirate of a man, who was so tough and strong and had been in more terrifying situations.

"You're not fine." He sounded irritated. Concerned.

Would he understand? She drew in a steady

breath. "Normally I'm so busy when I'm in flight that I don't notice how high up we really are."

"Afraid of heights?"

She nodded, struggling to push the memories back down into the compartment where she kept them, in a dark, sad place in her heart. When she opened her eyes, it was with the bump of the skids meeting the blessed earth.

Now, if she could only pretend she was all right. Because she was—what did she have to complain about? She was here and alive and with Sam. It was friendship that glowed between them as he killed the engine and reached for her hand. His touch was that of comfort and connection and she wanted more.

She wanted to reach out and sink into his arms. To lay her cheek against the comforting solid plane of his chest, and hold on forever. She longed for it more than anything. But what right did she have?

Guilt clenched like a vise tight around her heart, squeezing harder until it hurt to breathe. She shrugged away his touch and unlatched the seat harness.

If Sam knew, would he want her? Would he understand?

Her Mr. Perfect would. As she'd written on her list. The right man would love her anyway.

But was there such a man?

She wasn't sure. As her feet hit the ground, she glanced over her shoulder to see him looking so competent at the controls. Back straight, shoulders set, head bowed slightly forward as he scribbled in his flight log. He was a man with enough courage to have served their country and to serve his community, with strength and grace and humor.

No, he wouldn't understand. He would never understand.

She ran as fast as she could. She wanted to get away from him. She never wanted to see him again. So he wouldn't ask what had happened up there. And she wouldn't have to tell him, and he wouldn't have to know.

So he wouldn't see the real Kirby McKaslin. The Kirby no one knew.

No, it was better to run away and keep running.

"Kirby! Hey, wait up!" His booming voice sounded concerned.

She kept on going. Dug her keys out of her

pocket and hit the remote. Her lights flashed, the door was unlocked and all she had to do was yank it open and she'd be safe from him—

"Kirby. Hey, what's wrong?" A steely hand curled over her shoulder, pinning her in place before she could leap into her car. "Whatever I did, I'm sorry. I didn't know you were afraid of flying. Not really. I'd never meant to hurt you."

His warm breath tickled the side of her neck. His touch was both an undeniable claim and an offer of comfort.

The last thing she needed. Or deserved.

"I can't believe this. You're shaking. I can feel it. You weren't just afraid. You were terrified." His hand slid down from her shoulder to her wrist. "Your hands are cold. I don't understand."

"I'm sure you wouldn't. You said you've crashed twice and look at you. You're not afraid to fly."

"We're not talking about me."

"This is all about you, don't you see?" Did he have to be so caring? If he were less than perfect, then she wouldn't be here with her heart breaking and the past so tangible she could taste it. Hear it.

"What does that mean? If it's not the flight, then what did I do that's got you all upset? Tell me, Kirby. I need to know."

"You won't understand."

"I'm not the dimmest bulb in the pack, so give me some credit. I've got enough gray matter to understand, whatever it is. So just tell me."

She wanted to feel his iron-strong arms around her. She wanted to hold on to him and close her eyes and let this pain inside her go. To find peace and happiness and be able to say, finally, she'd been enough. Done enough.

But she wasn't. She hadn't. And if he knew—

He'd never love her. Never want her.

"You're killin' me, beautiful." As if he knew her secret wishes, he folded his powerful arms around her and nudged her to his chest. His hand cupped the back of her head, holding her safe and tender. It was more than physical closeness.

She could feel his heart. Strong and vulnerable and caring. Infinitely caring.

Tears pricked behind her eyes, sharp and hot. She would not give in, would not let herself hope. Not until he knew the truth, and then he'd turn away....

"Tell me." His voice vibrated through her, as if it were a part of her, as if he were already a part of her heart. "I need to know. I want to make this better."

Why did he have to be her dream come true? And how could she bear to lose him? His hand stroked the back of her head, tangling in her hair. His warm touch was awkward, slightly rough, as if this were new to him, too. But tender.

Tender enough to destroy the ice around her heart.

Leaving her open and vulnerable and more exposed than she'd been with anyone. Ever. "It's not your fault."

"I don't understand."

"You wouldn't." How could he? He was a hero by anyone's standards. So great and strong, good and decent and invincible. "You're not afraid. You're not afraid of anything."

"That's not true, darlin'. I've been afraid plenty of times."

"When?" she demanded. And when he didn't answer, she turned away.

This wasn't about going up in the helicopter

tonight. Sam figured he might as well fess up. "I've been afraid more than I've been not afraid, I'll tell you that. Is this about that medical flight going down a while ago? You had to have known the folks on board."

"I did. I know how it was for them."

Sam felt her go rigid. Her muscles tensed beneath his fingertips as he held her by the wrist. He felt her pain as if it were his own. He'd never known a connection like this before. He could feel her terror. Nurses saw a lot of trauma after the fact, in the battle to save lives.

Was that what was hurting her? Had she been on duty that night? "I've seen a lot of crashes—they're bad. No doubt about it. But know this. You are safe with me. I have my faults, but I'm a careful pilot."

"I believe in you, Sam." Her voice came muffled, and he felt her break then, the first shuddering sob, which came without tears. Pure emotion, pure pain.

Quaking now, she pulled away from him again.

He let her go. He knew about death. He knew about grieving. He knew about losses and images that haunted forever. "This is about your sister."

Kirby sagged against the side of her car. "I couldn't save her. I did everything. *Everything* I knew to do. There was nothing I could do—"

"You were on the flight?"

Tears shone in her eyes, but didn't fall. "I was a nurse, but I couldn't stop her from dying."

"I know how that feels." He put aside his own memories struggling to the surface. He put aside every emotion in him except the ones for Kirby. For Kirby who worked so hard, who did so much for others, who healed and comforted the sick.

He took her elbows, holding her up. "It's a helpless feeling."

"I did everything I knew. It wasn't enough." Tears shimmered but did not fall. "*I* wasn't enough."

"You were injured, too?"

Kirby turned away. How could she look into Sam's eyes? A strong man, a hero. He didn't let people down, the way she had.

After the accident, no one had said so. No one had ever hinted at it. Not in her family and not in her community. There had been two survivors that day, when a pilot's error during bad weather had brought the private plane crashing into the foothills of the Bridger Mountains. She'd been one of them.

When the search and rescue team had arrived, John Corey had pried her away from her sister's body. Kirby had never spoken from that day on about the pain of her own injuries or the terror of the crash, of struggling in pain and shock and confusion to try to save one dying person after another. With no supplies, no medical equipment, no help.

She never talked again about how Allison had died. By covering Kirby during the impact and saving her from the fire and the flying debris.

And later, no one had said a word. But she knew they wondered. Had she done enough? Could she have done more? And while there had never been any blame, she'd watched grief tear her family apart. Time was mending some of those rifts, but life in the McKaslin family had forever changed.

So had she.

The past could not be changed. It wasn't a tape to be recorded over or a movie take to be refilmed. And from that day forward, she'd done everything she could to make up for what had happened. She worked hard. She learned more. She volunteered. She rescued a puppy from the animal shelter.

It was never enough. How could it be?

How did she stop the pain gnawing at her heart like a hungry termite? Nibbling away on the edges so that the hurting never stopped? With every bite there was less of her, and she didn't know how to ever feel whole again.

And there stood Sam, as invincible as the night and so amazing and capable, he looked as if nothing could ever defeat him.

All he had to do was hold her, and he could ease this pain. In his arms she felt comforted. She needed him, in the deep places in her soul where no light reached.

"You did all you could. Sometimes that's the only truth there is. And you have to find a way to live with it." Tender, his words. Caring, his touch as he held her arms. When she planted her hands on his chest to push away, he stopped her. "Trust that you were there for a reason."

"What reason? I held her while she died, and what really mattered inside me died, too. And do you know the worst thing? Do you know what I did when the rescue team found us? My first thought was, I'm going to live."

There, she'd said it. "Now you know how petty I am."

He knew the worst of her. He wouldn't want her now. There was no way she was going to see that on his face. See his affection for her change to hatred.

But he didn't let her go. He pinned her to his chest and held her there. Tears scalded her eyes and came in a hot burning wave that drowned her. Tears of sorrow and horror and loss broke loose and crashed through her. Sorrow for the other people, wounded and broken, she couldn't save.

Sorrow for the pediatric floor nurse who had no trauma training, no emergency nursing. For her oldest sister she loved so fiercely and for her loss that would never be healed.

She cried because now that Sam knew, he couldn't stand her either.

She pushed away from Sam, and this time he let her go. She yanked open her door and he didn't stop her. She drove away, spitting gravel as she drove too fast, watching his image in her rearview mirror.

He stood bigger, taller. A man of substance and honor and courage, surrounded by the night, blessed by the silvered moonlight. As she rounded the corner, he disappeared from her sight.

The stars winked, bright and perfect, above the cemetery. Their light hazed down on the headstone of pure white marble. Carla would have approved. He was still healing the knee he'd blown out, the femur he'd broken in five places during the crash and the gunshot wounds from the fight with the enemy.

Now this new wound. She'd told him she'd never forgive him for letting Mark die, his navigator and his best friend. She'd been in love with Mark, but he'd rejected her. She'd married him only so she could be a pilot's wife. An officer's wife.

That was the greatest wound of all—inflicted when he'd come home to the wife he loved more than his life. He'd endured capture and torture and watching the deaths of his closest friends and held on with this steadfast faith and his unconditional love for his wife. The goodness that had helped him hold on in the face of cruelty.

All he'd wanted to do was love his wife. Have a good life with her. And she'd turned away from him. Blamed him. Told him she wanted a divorce and sped away, only to die in a car accident twelve minutes later.

She'd taken his heart with her to the grave. He felt as if the only light on this earth he'd believed in had been snuffed out.

And he was alone in the dark.

Sam startled awake to a silence that felt as thick as sorrow. His breathing, the rustle of the sheets as he flung them off, the groan of the mattress coils as he sat up to bury his face in his hands emphasized just how alone he really was.

Would it always be this way? And why, tonight, was he wondering that question? For the first time since the day he'd buried his wife, he wanted to love again. How insane was that? Her betrayals had cut him deeply and remained a scar on his soul.

Never trust a woman with too much of you. That's what he'd learned. He saw it over and over again over the years, with his buddies from high school and from the service. Marriages that didn't last, that couldn't stand the test of time. And many of those that lasted did so with sadness and distance for the children's sakes or because divorce was unthinkable.

This was Kirby's fault. She made him want to believe. She made him want to try. She made him wonder, what if this time with her it could be different?

Anger speared through him, both hot and sharp. The pain was a physical one that had him bounding up from the mattress and stumbling around a snoring Leo sprawled out on the floor. Sam yanked on his wrinkled pair of jeans as he stormed into the hallway.

She'd surprised him tonight. She'd rattled him. She'd knocked at the defenses surrounding his heart, and those defenses were holding...*barely*.

Yep, this was all her fault.

Tonight her house was dark. Had she come home? He'd driven straight from the airport, but her car wasn't in the driveway. Worried about her, he'd cruised through town but hadn't spotted her car parked along the main street. She had probably gone home to her family, he figured, or to one of those sisters of hers and some serious girl talk.

At least, that's what he hoped. The thought of her alone and hurting tore at him.

He'd kept an eye out for her lights next door, but she hadn't come home.

She doesn't need you, man. She had family. She had her pick of men more worthy than him. But he wanted to be the shoulder she leaned on. He wanted to be her shelter from the storms of her life. Why?

Because she'd made him feel. Strong. Worthy. Wanted. She'd clung to him, her fingers clenching the knit fabric of his T-shirt. She'd held him so tight. She needed him. *Him*. She'd felt so fragile and precious and—

Whoa, hold it right there, man. That's the kind of thinking that got you into trouble last time.

And what a mess of trouble that had turned out to be.

He padded through the kitchen, stole a root beer from the fridge and popped the top. The soda was ice-cold on his tongue and fizzled down his throat. But nothing would soothe him on this night, so he set it on the counter.

The clock on the stove said it was well after two. Was Kirby home? He couldn't see her driveway from this angle, and all her windows were dark. Wait, there was a movement. Outside, on her back porch.

Adrenaline shot through him. His first thought was a burglar. But no, it couldn't be. The shadow was too slim, and if it was a burglar, it was a very unambitious one. It was a woman, her long hair tumbling over her shoulders as she eased onto the top porch step. She hid her face in her hands, a perfect image of misery.

Kirby.

Chapter Eleven

The fence boards groaned. It was Kirby's only warning before a dark shock of hair and two eyes peered over the top of the boards. Sam climbed over the fence like an escaped prisoner, or maybe a spy on a mission, and landed upright, on both feet. The little spaniel gave a yip of greeting and ran over to wiggle in a circle around Sam's ankles.

"Can't you use the gate like a normal person?"

"Why be normal?"

She rolled her eyes. She should have known she couldn't escape him. That's why she hadn't come straight home. Why she'd driven around the countryside for a while, thought about heading to her parents' house and decided against it. In the end, she wanted to be alone.

And still did.

Thank goodness it was dark. She didn't think she could look Sam Gardner in the eye. She stood and dusted off her sweats. "C'mon, Jessie, time for bed."

The spaniel refused to come, preferring to orbit Sam's ankles. Sam's big hands looked rough, but they were gentle as he knelt to stroke the dog's back. Steady and caring.

Mr. Perfect.

Why did that suddenly make her angry? Kirby fought a quick wave of despair. There was no way he'd treat her the same way. No chance that he'd pull her against his chest and hold her close forever.

There was no chance of being wrapped in his arms and finding hope. As if she could finally start living again.

That didn't make any sense, because she *was* living, she *was* alive. She had her own house and a perfectly useful life. She volunteered and worked and was faithful. She tried to be a good daughter and sister.

"You're not okay. Don't lie me." Sam's touch grazed her face, drying away a tear.

She wasn't crying. She blinked hard to

keep the emotions dammed up where they belonged. "I'll *be* all right."

"That's not good enough. Sorry. You need a friend, and here I am."

A friend. Yeah, that's what she needed. "I have plenty of friends."

She turned away, fighting a suffocating sorrow that was pulling her down. She needed to be alone. She wanted to get away from Sam so he wouldn't see what a mess she really was.

"Bet you don't have a friend like me." He brushed windswept hair from the side of her face, exposing her more to him.

Exposing too much. Panic welled up, too.

Choking, she stumbled away.

"I'm not going to leave until I know you're all right." His step sounded on the deck behind her.

Kirby felt his closeness like a radiant heat. Felt it like a brush to her heart. Like a comfort to her soul.

"I told you, I'm fine." She squeezed her eyes shut against the memories. The images of what a plane crash could do. Of blood and horror and fire.

"Liar." He curled his fingers around her nape, his fingertips skimming the skin an inch below her collar. "Scars from a fire. You were burned."

She nodded. "Half of my back. It wasn't bad. It wasn't anything compared to—" She took a few deep breaths. Nothing hurt more than the emotional pain. The horror of that night. And the guilt of every day since.

He wanted to ease her pain. "I was flying in to pick up a team of SEALs on a black ops mission and took a direct hit. There was nothing I could do. Next thing I knew, my bird was smoking. I had no controls and we were dropping. We hit hard. I mean, I did everything I could and it was a bad impact. I couldn't believe the three of us were still alive. We were all busted up real good."

"Did people die?"

"Yeah. And why not me? I lived. I was hurtin' bad, but the luck of the draw, the way the bird went down, I had no control, nothin'. We hit trees or we would all have been dead. I think of that crash nearly every day of my life."

"You were a good soldier, too, weren't you?"

"Passable. Good enough that we put up a good fight before we ran out of ammo."

"You were hurt?"

"Yeah."

She heard the sadness in his voice, the honesty. See how noble Sam was?

Her voice cracked with the respect she felt for him. "You were captured?"

"Yep."

She went cold. He'd had it so much worse than she could ever imagine. "You were rescued?"

"I was. But my buddies died and there was nothing I could do. To this day I feel responsible, but I can't go back and change anything. Sometimes bad things happen. It's hard to accept, but it's true. And when things go wrong, all we can do is our best to deal with it."

Hot tears crept down her cheeks. "I'm sorry your friends died."

"Me, too." His voice cracked, raw and thick with emotion. "I had the privilege of living, of going home to the wife I loved more than my life and attending my friends' funerals. Men who died while I survived."

"I know how that feels." She wanted to wrap her arms around him and take his pain. To do anything to keep him from hurting. But what right did she have? He was not hers to love.

He never would be.

Sam cleared his throat and stared up at the stars so crisp and bright. "That's why I retired. I couldn't bury any more buddies. Living is better than dying, but it sure is harder. It took me a long time before I figured out I still had a life. And it dishonored their memories if I didn't do my best every day to enjoy my second chance."

"But you were a hero."

"No, I'm just a man, Kirby."

"I was a nurse. I couldn't make a difference." She couldn't ever forget.

Or forgive herself. So how could he forgive her?

"All those people you couldn't help." Sam could feel her pain as if it were his own. He knew about guilt. He knew about sorrow so deep it reached clear to the soul. "Don't blame yourself. You did all you could."

How could he be so kind? He knew the worst about her. The very worst. She wasn't a good person. Not at all. "I should have done something. The injuries were too critical. I—I can't talk about this. C'mon, Jess. We're going in."

Sam's words stopped her. "Maybe you were

in that plane on that day for a different reason. Maybe you weren't meant to save them."

"No, I can't accept that I let people who were good and kind die. I was supposed to help them. I'm a nurse. I've been called to be a nurse, and on the day it mattered, I failed them. I failed myself."

There. It was only the truth. Shame crashed through her with the force of an ocean wave, knocking her off balance, and she lurched toward the door.

As often as she prayed, she'd never found any comfort. Any answer. Any solution other than to keep trying to be a better nurse. To hope one day she would make a difference.

"Or maybe you weren't there to save them, Kirby. But to comfort them in an impossible situation."

"But I couldn't—"

"Maybe you were there to be a comfort to your sister and to those you've known all your life, when they needed comfort most of all."

That could *not* be true. Kirby leaned her forehead against the glass pane in the door, her hand at the knob. She stood perfectly still, but she was breaking inside. "I was no comfort to anyone, I'm sure."

"Yeah? You make a difference every day.

I've seen you at work. I know the kind of person you are, Kirby. You shouldn't feel guilty. You should feel glad you were there where you were needed. You need to take responsibility for what you did, not for what you were never responsible for. You cared for the dying. You did what you could to ease their suffering."

There had been so much suffering. She'd felt so inadequate to the task that day.

"You're a good, gentle soul, and that makes a difference, Kirby. Maybe it is the only difference we can really make in this world. To be kind and compassionate. To love."

She felt as if she were crumbling from the inside out. The hard wall she'd put up around the wounds in her spirit, to hide all her fears and shame, was cracking. Sam's gentle baritone punched at those defenses, and they were coming down. Every last one.

Like a breached dam, all those pent-up feelings and stored-up pain cascaded free, moving through her, falling away.

"Let it go, Kirby." He folded his arms around her middle, supporting her so that her back was to his chest. So secure, holding her up when her knees wobbled.

"It's okay," he told her. "Just let go. Let it go."

"I can't."

"You have to." His lips brushed the crown of her head in a tender kiss. "Or it will consume you until it's taken everything valuable about your life."

"Maybe that's the way it should be."

"And what good is that gonna do you? Or those people you couldn't save? Is that why you were spared? So you could live in the past, trying to correct something that was never your fault? Or would your sister want you to embrace all that's good in life and keep making a difference in this world?"

"That's what I'm trying to do. I volunteer—"

"For the wrong reasons. And that makes all the difference." He kissed her cheek, a warm brush of sweetness. Of caring.

Of love? she wondered.

"It's late." He released her. "Let's get you inside."

He opened the door and her dog dashed in first, anxious over Kirby's distress.

Sam moved past her in the dark kitchen, found her box of dog biscuits on the counter and handed one to her spaniel. "You were a good girl," he told Jessie. "Go to bed, go on."

With a look of uncertainty the dog glanced at Kirby, whined and then obeyed, trotting down the short hall and disappearing into the nearby bedroom.

"You're next." Sam took her by the hand, commanding but gentle.

How could a man be so strong and tender at once? She admired him even more as he led her down the hall, set her on the edge of her bed and knelt to tug off her shoes. The love she felt for him doubled inside her. Tripled. Expanded until she brimmed full with it, a bright pure light of affection that hurt as much as it healed.

"You be smart and listen to me, because I'm right about this. I promise." He gently nudged her shoulder, guiding her down to her pillows, and tucked the covers up to her chin. "Let go and sleep, okay?"

How was she going to defend herself against him now? He'd stolen her heart. She loved him with all of her being. With all her soul.

His kiss grazed her lips. Warm as velvet, gentle as mercy, as thrilling as first love.

As true love.

"Sleep well, beautiful. I'll see you tomorrow."

She couldn't speak. She was too raw. Too drained. She could only watch as he moved through the darkness, substance and shadow. He closed the door behind him, leaving her alone.

But not lonely.

Sam was the one. The one she was meant to love forever and for all time.

Sam watched dawn take over the sky and decided to get up from the front step and make a pot of coffee. Strong enough to keep even him awake. He had a long day of work ahead. The accountant was going to go over the books with him, and that was scary. He was going to have to figure out how to keep up with the paperwork or hire a bookkeeper to do it.

The thought of sharing the quiet of his office with anyone, especially a woman, made him decide that he'd rather learn to do it himself. After all, he was a businessman. He ought to be able to figure out the books.

Leo trotted into the kitchen, yawned and looked pointedly at his bowl.

"Here you go, boy." Sam filled the dog bowl with kibbles.

While Leo ate as through he'd been starving, gobbling and crunching and gulping, Sam grabbed the bag of coffee from the freezer. It took less than a minute to get a pot brewing, and the warm comforting scent encouraged him. He might make it through the day to come.

Sleep had eluded him. Why? He hadn't been haunted by the past in his dreams. He'd been up thinking about Kirby. No, he'd been trying *not* to think about Kirby.

He'd worried about her. He was concerned about her. He cared about her. About Miss Perfect In Every Way.

He grabbed his favorite mug off the drainer and filled it with steaming coffee. Leaving the rest of the pot to brew, he headed to the front door. Kirby was probably up by now, letting her little dog into the backyard. He wanted to check on her, but his feelings were too raw.

He needed to figure out how he felt about her before he saw her again. He needed to know how to act. Everything had consequences, and last night he'd kissed her. He winced. He loved kissing her. He hadn't meant to kiss her. It had simply happened.

"C'mon Leo." He yanked open the front door, deciding to avoid her.

Whatever he was feeling, he wanted to get it straightened out before he saw her again. It was the smart thing to do.

Except he should have checked out his window first. There she was, looking like everything good in the world, standing in her front yard. She wore a modest blue sweater and black pants, and her hair was unbound, soft and shimmering and glorious.

She was beautiful. More so today than he'd ever seen her. How was it that she grew more lovely every time he looked at her?

Leo barked and bounded down the front steps, and it was too late to do anything but follow him out into the bright sunshine. The little spaniel gave a yip in greeting and the dogs sniffed noses, then took off running around the front yard together.

"I'm running late this morning," he explained as he knelt to grab his morning paper from the sidewalk. "How about you? How did you sleep?"

"Good. I start at seven this morning." She pushed up her sleeve to glance at her gold watch. "I've got to get going. Thank you for last night, Sam. For everything you did."

"My pleasure, ma'am."

He wanted to brush the soft hair from her face, the golden strands that shone like the sun and whipped in cadence with the wind. He wanted to use those errant strands as an excuse to run his fingers along the curve of her face, to feel her satin skin, to hold her again, if only for one brief moment.

"I've got to go. I wish I had more time. Hey, maybe it's my turn to cook you dinner?" She snapped her slim fingers and her dog came running.

Sam felt a bubble of panic rise in his chest. He was panicking because he liked the idea. A lot. How wrong was that? "I've got a late night at work."

"Oh, and I'm meeting with some friends tonight. What am I thinking?" She tossed him a megawatt smile, the kind that a woman gave a man she really cared about.

"Hey, another time, then." At least that would give him time to think this through.

"Sure. Have a good day, Sam. Bye, Leo." She grabbed her spaniel's leash and headed up the walkway. "See you later."

"Yeah."

Sam sank to his bottom porch step and set down the mug before he spilled his coffee.

What was this he was feeling for her? It was like nothing he'd ever known before.

He was lonely, that was it. He was getting soft in his old age, now that he was over thirty, and it was hard living alone. He didn't deny that. But it was better than the alternative.

Kirby would make a loving wife. That thought came out of the blue, a whisper in his ear, and it troubled him more.

By the time he'd sipped his way to the bottom of the oversize mug, there she was, backing out of her driveway, looking carefully over her shoulder as she eased out onto the street.

She waved before she put her car in gear and drove away.

Leaving a hole the size of Montana in his chest.

"Okay, we want the scoop." Michelle pounced on her the instant she set foot inside the coffee shop, where their informal support group met once a month.

Kirby shrugged out of her coat and hung it on the old-fashioned coat rack by the door.

The coffee shop was closed to regular customers this time of night, but Michelle had been busy, whipping up frothy drinks for the handful of women seated cozily around a table in the corner by the windows. Why was everyone staring at her like that?

"Tell us about this handsome man you've been secretly dating." Alexandra Corey adjusted her three-month-old son in her arms. "A very handsome and rich man, I hear."

"Sam's handsome, if you like tall, dark and rugged." Kirby kept her voice neutral as she slipped into the last empty chair at the table. "But I don't think he's rich."

Everyone broke out in laughter.

"Yeah, sure, he buys an airport. He has two helicopters and a Cessna." Michelle rolled her eyes. "I think he's really poor to afford all that. Here's a vanilla steamer, sister dear. Tell us how long you've been dating that eligible bachelor behind our backs? The whole time? Or did he just start asking you out?"

Kirby would have thanked her sister for the coffee, but she was not happy to be embarrassed. "I'm not dating Sam. We're neighbors. We're friends."

"Friends, huh?" Michelle plopped into her chair beside Kirby. "Is he, like, in love with you yet? Do you love him?"

"No!"

"A little defensive, are you, sister dear?"

It was true. She loved Sam more than she thought could be possible. All day long she'd felt a longing she'd never known before. The steady burning light inside her remained, unconditional and never ending.

The kind of love she'd always prayed to find, and it was more than she'd ever expected.

And last night Sam had comforted her when she'd needed it. He'd held her close when she'd felt so utterly alone. He'd tucked her into bed with the care and respect of the greatest of heroes when she didn't feel as if she deserved it.

When she looked at him, she saw his strength, his goodness and his great heart.

She felt as if she glowed, from head to toe, from skin to soul, simply thinking of him. She ached with the wish to see him again.

In a few hours, she thought. She'd be home and so would he. The evening was a warm one, with the hint of summer on the breeze. Suddenly she could see her future spread out before her. One of hope. Of goodness.

Of love.

Chapter Twelve

Who invented the computer and thought it was a good idea? Sam wanted to know. He resisted the urge to grab the contraption, and the printer, too, and hurl it out the open window.

This computer program is so easy that you'll be able to do all your bookkeeping yourself, the CPA had promised.

Easy? What was easy about this? Sam had a degree in physics. He had brazened into hostile territory nap of the earth—so low, they bellied treetops the entire mission. He'd flown birds that were shot at, shot up, on fire, barely working and not working at all.

He'd survived being captured. He'd flown all over the world. He'd handled all that without batting an eye.

But not this frustrating plastic box some people called a computer. The apparatus sat mocking him in his own kitchen.

"What do you mean there's no printer?" Maybe talking sense to the machine would help. "It's hooked up right here. See? It's the right cable. Fits nice and tight. The power is on. So just print. Aghh!"

Leo nudged his nose against Sam's hand in sympathy. The dog's chocolate-brown eyes were sorrowful, as if he shared the same opinion about that suspicious computer.

Time to take a break. Maybe the computer would have a change of heart and decide to open up friendly negotiations with the printer. If not, then Sam intended to call the CPA and beg for help.

"Yoo-hoo, is anybody home?" His aunt's cheerful voice echoed through the house.

The tension drained away, and Sam gladly stormed from the kitchen to yank open the screen door. "Aren't you a welcome sight? And a lovely one."

"Oh, you flatterer." Ruth drew his face down to plant a maternal kiss on his cheek. "Keep those compliments coming. At my age, I'll take all of them I can get. Goodness, what changes you've made in this place!"

"Yep, I just put in the vinyl windows."

"So I see." Ruth ran her fingers over the wood frames he'd carefully nailed into their original place. "What a fine job you've done. Although with you, I wouldn't expect anything less. Oh, you're too thin. You're losing weight cooking for yourself."

"I'm the same weight I always am, and I'm a good cook. You know that."

"I know, but I've read time and time again how a man is happier and lives longer if he's married."

"Really? I figured marriage would be so stressful for us poor men, it would kill us faster." He winked.

"Oh, you stop that now!" Laughing, Ruth held out her arms and he braced himself. He knew more doting affection was coming, and he was helpless to stop it.

Best to just give in, don't struggle. It would be over faster.

"I love you and want what's best for you, my boy," she said, her voice wobbly with affection as she wrapped her frail arms around his middle and squeezed him tight.

Ah, it was good to have a family again.

"You're the closest thing I have to a son, so indulge me. Get married and be happy."

"I tried that. I wasn't happy."

Ruth stepped away, and when she did, sorrow for him shone in her eyes. "I know. It was wrong how Carla treated you. You didn't deserve that."

He felt his insides turn steely cold. "I try not to think about that time in my life. You know that."

"Yes, but I must point out that not every woman is selfish. There are plenty of good women on this planet who have big hearts and love deeply. I was one of them."

"I know, Ruth. That's why I think you're the greatest woman I know. My uncle was lucky to have you."

"The love I had for my Ned was the sweetest part of my life. I miss him something terrible, but the years we had, my, what a comfort that is. Marriage can be bliss. Believe me, I know. Which reminds me, I heard a rumor about you taking little Kirby McKaslin out on a date."

"We happened to both wind up at the burger place and shared a table. Did everyone in this town drive by that night and see us? Inviting her to share my table was the polite and gentlemanly thing to do. I was showing off the one good manner I have."

"Oh, you are impossible!" Ruth lifted her chin, looking as if she'd already made up her mind and no one was going to change it, and marched into the kitchen. "What have you done in here? Oh, my. You bought a computer."

"You mean a box of torture, frustration and misery?"

"Having a few problems with it, are you? You mean there's one thing in this world that Sam Gardner can't do perfectly?" Ruth had the audacity to look delighted as she rubbed her hands together, looking over the computer with glee. "Oh, this is a nice system. Let's see what your problem is."

"Wait a minute. You know something about computers?"

"Why, of course. I Internet all the time. There are so many wonderful things! I belong to a book club online, can you imagine? We read inspirational romances and discuss them. Oh, and the book resources and, my, those lists. I belong to a rubber-stamping list and a crocheting one, and I could go on and on. Look, I see what your problem is. I'll just change this setting."

To Sam's complete amazement, the printer

that had remained stubbornly silent started printing. "You're a lifesaver."

"No more than you are, my boy." Ruth glanced up, and her sharp gaze traveled straight to the window that looked out over the neighboring backyard. "Kirby is home. Isn't she just a lovely girl?"

Sam prayed for patience. He was going to need it. "Of course she is, but no one is as lovely as you."

"Stop that, now. Goodness, I'm trying to open your eyes to the love of—"

"Pizza? It's nearly suppertime. I could phone in an order to the local pizza place."

"Pizza is not love."

"It is if you're hungry."

"Oh, how you make me laugh. You're too much like your uncle. My side is starting to hurt." She waggled her finger at him. "I'm talking about love. You've been alone a long time. Maybe you ought to let go of the past. Maybe what's ahead of you, if you are man enough to risk it, will be the best part of your life. You never know."

"All right, I hear you. I've listened. Now, can we change the subject? Why did you stop by, anyway?"

"I just got lonely for you and wanted to see

for myself if this house is going to suit you. There's more damage here than you told me about—"

"Yes, but don't you worry about it. Since I'm not ever going to marry, I have a lot of time on my hands. I like to work with tools. Saws. Drills. Hammers. It completes me as a man."

Ruth held her stomach as she howled. Good, he liked making her laugh. She'd been sad for a long time after Ned's death. "Fine. Do you know how to run this computer? Or do you need someone to show you?"

"What will it cost me?"

Ruth set her big black handbag on the table and pulled up a chair. She didn't look altruistic at all as she named her price. "I want to see a wedding ring on your hand by summer's end."

"No deal. The offer of a pizza still stands."

"Then I'll take it, but I'm not giving up hope for you, my boy." She patted his hand, a lifetime of love, of family ties, strong between them.

The keyboard tapped as Ruth worked, and Sam tried to pay attention. He really did. He wanted to figure out the computer so he didn't have to rely on anyone.

He was a loner. A survivor. A strong man who didn't need love.

So why did his gaze drift to the window? Why did his attention turn from the monitor's bright screen to the woman next door? Why did his chest squeeze and his soul fill with peace? Why did longing move through him at the sight of her? At the sight of her graceful, gentle beauty. At the memory of having her in his arms, so sweet and soft and lovely.

Why was it, when he looked at her, he felt whole? As if the past wounds no longer hurt. As if Carla and her memory no longer mattered.

He could almost imagine it. Kirby turning toward him with real love in her eyes, reaching out to him, the man she loved honest and true. She could light up his life, like dawn to the world.

Did he have enough heart left to love her in return? The pit in the center of his chest was cold. Hard. Broken.

What was he doing? He had no business letting the wish into his heart. The wish for her.

Unaware he was watching from the window,

Kirby flicked a long shank of her wavy hair behind her shoulder and pulled something from her pocket. A plastic pink ball. She held it up for her dog to see and then tossed it. The ball sailed through the air, the spaniel barked happily in pursuit and Kirby clapped her hands, cheering on her beloved dog as the cocker retrieved the ball and ran back to her mistress.

Kirby knelt, praising the animal gently, and brushed her fingertips across the dog's soft curls. So loving and gentle. What a good wife she would make, he realized. What a wonderful mom.

She deserved so much. What she didn't need was someone who was cynical and wounded and used up. A man who was tarnished by life. Who would always be.

Kirby deserved a man with a whole heart to give her. A man who believed there was love on this earth strong enough to last.

And if it made him sad, made him feel as if the bottom had just dropped out of his world, well, then, that was just the way it was. He was a realist. He was tough. He was strong enough to make the right decisions.

"How about that pizza, Ruth? You like double pepperoni and sausage, right?"

"You'd better make it a large. I'm hungry." Hope twinkled in her eyes.

Sam groaned. He knew, beyond a doubt, that she'd seen his heart on his face. Saw his tender feelings for Kirby McKaslin that he refused to name.

Refused to feel.

Was it her imagination or was Sam busier than he'd been for weeks? Kirby wondered as she rinsed vegetables in her sink. She spotted Leo racing around in the backyard, sniffing the air, checking for invaders or for squirrels that were hiding in the trees.

But no sign of Sam.

She'd hoped to catch up to him this evening. She'd kept an eye out for him, thinking he might step out onto his back deck to barbecue his supper. But it didn't look as though he was anywhere near. His windows were closed up tight. His truck wasn't in the driveway.

She'd held off fixing her own meal in the hopes that Sam would come home. Her stomach growled.

"That's what I get for waiting." For wanting. She turned the lettuce upside down to drain, left the carrot and tomato in the drainer and plugged in her grilling machine. She didn't feel like making a fuss over lighting up the barbecue. She'd be making a meal for one, like always.

But maybe not forever.

She grabbed the spatula and lifted the beef patty onto the grill. She seasoned the beef, lowered the grill's lid and washed her hands in the sink. And because the window just happened to be in front of her, she looked through it and noticed Sam still wasn't home.

She missed him. An entire day and a half had gone by and she hadn't seen him. She longed for him. Remembered the way he'd kissed her tenderly. She felt thrilled and alive, as if everything was right in the world. As if nothing would ever be wrong again.

The phone rang. Was it Sam? She still had time to throw another patty on the grill. Hope uplifted her as she snatched the cordless from the table and glanced at the caller ID.

Not Sam, but Kendra. Kirby tamped down her disappointment, because it was always good to hear from her sister. "Howdy, stranger."

"I've been thinking about you, so I thought I'd give you a call." Kendra was a year older than Kirby, and they had always been close.

"You left first last night. I didn't get the chance to talk to you. Nobody did."

"I know. I had to head home and take care of my dog."

"Sure. If I were Michelle, I'd say that you were rushing home to spend time with that new neighbor of yours."

Kirby groaned. "No, I don't want to talk about it—"

"But I'm not Michelle, so I understand. Just take your time, okay, sis? Falling in love means trusting someone. It's good to know he's worth that level of trust."

"Sam is a good man. I know it."

"Then you do care for him?"

"Yes." More than care. It was frightening, because it was so powerful. Nothing had ever felt so right. As if all the pieces of her life suddenly fit.

While she toasted the hamburger bun in the oven and removed the meat from the grill she asked how her sister's land purchase was progressing. By the time her sister had finished answering, Kirby had her hamburger made and was making up a small bowl of salad.

"Will I see you on Friday, or will you have a big date?" Kendra asked.

"I'll let you know right after I know." Kirby

swept the last of the tomato from the cutting board into the bowl. "Otherwise, we're on for Friday night."

"Great. I love being your backup." Teasing, Kendra said goodbye and hung up.

Jessie barked the exact minute a knock rattled the glass window on her back door.

Sam. Kirby came alive at the sight of him. Every sense, every feeling inside her focused solely on him. Happiness made her feel weightless as she floated to the door. Leo pushed his way in, greeted the little spaniel and headed straight for her counter and her dog biscuits.

"Leo! Don't you dare," Sam ordered and glowered at his dog.

The big rottweiler sighed, gazed longingly at the treats, then at the hamburger sitting on the edge of the island.

"Don't even think about it. Come here. Lie down." Sam winked at Kirby, keeping a stern face for his errant dog. He waited while Leo ambled outside and lay down on the deck. The cocker joined him, snuggling up to him companionably in the late-evening sunshine. "Good dogs."

Kirby loved everything about this man. His sense of humor, the way he treated his dog.

The fact that seeing him was more thrilling than if someone handed her a million dollars cash. She loved the way his hard mouth softened in the corners and crooked upward when he started to grin.

Except he wasn't grinning. He looked tense, instead of relaxed. Pensive, instead of glad to see her. He glanced nervously at her prepared meal.

"Maybe I'd better come back. After you've had a chance to have your dinner."

"Why don't you come in anyway?" Whatever was wrong, maybe he wanted to talk about it. Maybe she could help him. After all, their relationship was deepening. She headed toward the refrigerator. "I bought the kind of root beer you like. Want one?"

"Uh, thanks." He jammed his hands into his jeans pockets. "So, you had a long day?"

"Pretty good. It was busy at work, but I wasn't the only practitioner on today, so I got home at a decent hour."

"And you're just now getting to your supper?"

"I was doing other things." A faint blush stained her face as she pulled open the refrigerator door and withdrew a can from the bottom shelf.

Sam caught a glimpse of her perfectly clean refrigerator, every item inside neat and orderly and in place. Just like the rest of her house. And her life.

A neat, orderly, pretty life he'd never fit into. Just say it and get this over with. He didn't want to, but he was man enough to face it.

And man enough to recognize the glow of emotion in Kirby's gaze as she handed him the cold can. How was he going to do this while she was eating? This wasn't the kind of pleasant conversation people had over dinner.

Her delicate brows furrowed. "Are you hungry? It will take a second to cook a burger on the grill."

"Thanks, but I took my aunt out to pizza."

"Ruth?" Kirby lifted her plate from the corner of the island. "How is she doing?"

"Better than I am. She taught me how to use my computer this afternoon. The one I bought and wanted to shove right back into the box about two minutes after I'd hooked it up."

"That's natural. Not to worry, because intense frustration is to be expected. They

don't tell you that in the instruction manual."
She glimmered like a pearl when she smiled.
A soft sheen of light that was gentle. Real.
True.

This was going to kill him.

The last thing he'd ever want to do was to
hurt Kirby.

He took the chair across from her. Sat
down, then popped the top of the aluminum
can, trying to figure out how best to start.

He already knew how this was going to
end. With Kirby hurt. How was he going to
stand that?

Chapter Thirteen

He took a long slow drink of soda. What was he waiting for? Might as well jump right in. No sense in letting this take longer than it needed to. It had to be done. He had to explain that he didn't want to mislead her. He wanted her to understand the way things were.

So, how did he start? "Talking with Ruth today got me to thinking. She's the only family I have left. The only family I'm likely to have."

Kirby sprinkled fat-free ranch dressing on her salad. "It must have been hard being away from your family, first in the military and then as a corporate pilot."

"Yep. By that time, my mom had passed. That left my wife, and my uncle and aunt. Now just my aunt."

"That's why you moved here. To be near her."

"Don't admit that to her, though. I'd never hear the end of it. She'd be stopping by constantly to kiss me on the cheek and show me how she's better on my computer than I'll ever be."

There he was, joking when he had serious business to do.

How could he do it? Kirby was so nice. So good and wonderful, everything a man could wish for. She was a dream come true.

But she couldn't be his dream.

It was better to stop this now, before they both got hurt.

"My aunt seems to think I might get married one day." Sam peered over the rim of his can as he took another long sip, watching Kirby's reaction. "Ruth's wrong, and having her talk on about me getting remarried makes me pretty uncomfortable. I'll never do that again. Ever."

Kirby stiffened. Her fingers tightened on the dressing bottle she held over her salad.

He hated this. He clenched his fists hard, looking at his white knuckles. "She thinks because she had a rare, happy marriage that everyone has that kind of relationship. I never told you about my wife, did I?"

Kirby put the dressing bottle down. Eyes big, she shook her head.

He could read so many emotions in those big luminous eyes of hers. Everything from surprise to a sad acceptance. What shocked him was the hard punch of emotion in his chest. He felt as if he were losing something, too, and felt the sorrow of it.

He cleared his throat and thought about leaving it at that. Maybe that had been enough for Kirby to get the idea. But he realized he had more to tell her. He owed her the truth. The whole of it.

Tenderness warred with the sadness inside him, because he really could love her.

"Remember I told you that I was captured? And two of my buddies died?"

Kirby didn't answer. She watched him with unblinking eyes, sitting so still that she didn't appear to be breathing.

"I was in pretty bad shape for Mark's funeral, but I made sure they let me out of the hospital to attend. And what a blessing *and* a curse, it turned out. My wife broke down after the service. Come to find out, she'd been in love with Mark, who had married someone else. She blamed me for his death. She'd never loved me. I never figured it out until that moment."

"You must have been devastated." Kirby closed her eyes, the crash flashing back to her in a quick, consuming horror. "You weren't responsible. You survived because you did, and to blame you—that makes no sense. It's not right. You're a good man, Sam. If you could have saved your friends, you would have done it."

"At any cost." He still felt that way. "Sound familiar?"

"Oh." She stared at the plate in front of her, her untouched food.

Well, maybe this would help her, too, in more than one way. "She'd broken places in my heart I didn't know were there. Places that have never healed to this day." He pushed away from the table. It hurt too much to remember. Tore at him as he headed to the door.

Finish it, Gardner. You can do it.

He took a steadying breath. Did what he had to do. "I think she was a very unhappy person inside, you know? She was never content with me or the life she'd been given. She always wanted something better. And she figured out pretty quick that I wasn't better. I come with flaws and failures and sorrows. I have no heart left to give. So, now you know the truth about me, Kirby."

"Who could be better than you, Sam?"

Kirby's gentle words, shining with sincerity, made his eyes burn. Carla, his own wife, had never said anything so kind. So caring.

And he hungered for it. Needed it so badly.

If only he could go back in time and choose Kirby instead, to come to her with a whole heart, to be the kind of man she needed.

But a man couldn't change his past. Or find his heart once it was lost. Who could love a man like that?

Not even Kirby, with her tenderhearted concern. With her good deeds and kindness.

It was better to save his pride and what remained of his dignity.

Sam couldn't look at Kirby. She would reach out and try to comfort him, and what good would come from that? It would only make him want her more.

So he walked off her porch and out of her life.

Sam disappeared before she could call out to stop him. He'd hopped over the deck rail and circled the corner of the house before she could race after him. Did she follow him home to make sure he was all right? Or did she respect the intent of his visit?

The ringing phone distracted her. She grabbed the receiver, then recognized the number on the display. Her upset and worry over Sam evaporated as she heard the dispatch from the emergency operator. The flight she'd agreed to staff was on. Sarah had a bone marrow donor.

Every instinct Kirby had made her want to say, "Call the next nurse on your list." But no, she would see this through. With Sarah. And with Sam.

By the time she'd called in her dog, locked the back door, made sure the grill was unplugged and grabbed her medical bag, Sam was backing his big pickup down his driveway and into the shadowed street.

So now you know the truth about me, Kirby. Yes, she knew the truth about Sam Gardner, but it wasn't what he thought. She saw a man deeply hurt. A man who didn't think he was lovable. Or able to love.

A man who didn't love her. He didn't want her.

Pain leveled her. At least she'd never told

him her true feelings. Embarrassed, shaken, she climbed into her car. She was in no mood for music, so she turned off the radio.

What Sam had said tonight proved he suspected how she was feeling.

She still had her pride. That was something. As much as she wanted to give in to the pain of her disappointment, the pain she felt on Sam's behalf was greater.

She carried around more guilt and sorrow than she could face over a past she could not change. But Sam seemed to be hurting even more. How deep did his wounds go? Would they ever heal?

She'd lost her dreams. Secret ones she'd never even realized she had until now. What his proposal would be like. What ring he would buy her. How it would feel to walk down the church aisle and see him waiting at the altar to make her his wife.

Troubled, she worried as she drove. How was she going to face him tonight, or ever again, and keep her heart from breaking even more?

Sarah needed her, and there was no way Kirby could hide in the car all night. She turned off the sedan's headlights, pocketed her car keys and grabbed her medical bag from the backseat. Her chest felt heavy, and it was hard to breathe as she headed toward Sam's helicopter.

How had she been so wrong? She'd been sure he loved her. Certain of his caring for her.

Luckily he was busy with his preflight check and, with his back to her, didn't see her as she climbed on board.

All she had to do was be professional. After all, she and Sam volunteered together. They were neighbors. So, she'd fallen in love with him. Well, she'd fall right back out. They would never again be friends, but they could be friendly.

Sam popped in through the side door, slammed it tight into place and locked it. Simply seeing him made pain rip through the center of her chest.

She was only lying to herself. Friendly?

She still loved him. She filled up from the bottom of her soul to the top of her heart from simply being near him.

What was she going to do? There was no future, she knew. There would be no dating and no proposing. No wedding and no happily-ever-after. *That's* what he'd told her tonight, in his own way.

He didn't want her enough. He didn't want to risk loving anyone again.

Sam stared at his clipboard, talking to her as if she were a stranger. "The doc is hiking south of Glacier. They got him on his cell and he's driving in to the local airstrip. We'll pick up him first, then head east for the girl."

Kirby nodded. Sam looked miserable. His eyes were shadowed and sad.

There was no spirit to him as he studied the clipboard so he didn't have to look at her. "They're tracking a storm just west of us. I'm going to try to swing around it, but it's supposed to be a slow mover. I might catch a little turbulence, so make sure you stay belted in."

"Fine." Was this how it was going to be between them? Strained? As if strangers?

Suddenly Kirby realized the risk she'd taken and knew she was feeling the price of it. Gone was the companionship she'd felt with Sam. The easygoing connection that had sparked between them, like the stars in a night sky, crisp and pure and inspiring.

But she'd lost more than his valuable friendship. She'd lost the love of her life. She'd never felt this way about any man. She knew, beyond a doubt, she never would again. Sam was special. He matched something in her soul, and she couldn't say what it was or how it was. It just was.

The *whop-whop* of the blades had her gripping her seat. The rotors whined, the ground gave way and the helicopter shot up into the sky. It was a queasy feeling, to know only thin strips of metal were keeping her safely up in the sky.

Sam was a good pilot, and she trusted him.

She trusted him with her life.

The flight would take a while, so Kirby pulled a book from her bag. She turned the paperback to the dog-eared page and read in the glow off the running lights.

But the words were meaningless. She really didn't feel like reading. Not with her mind spinning and her heart aching with Sam's words. *My aunt seems to think I might get married one day. I'll never do that again. Ever.*

Surely there was a chance. There was always a chance. Maybe if—

She caught herself. Couldn't believe she was thinking this way. Sam had made it clear. He didn't want to marry her.

There was no way to fix this. No way to

heal this. For once she had to accept something the way it was, not try to take responsibility for it and make it right.

Sam didn't feel the same way about her. It was that simple. And he was telling her how his wife had married him without really loving him, and the disaster that had brought them both.

No, marriage was a serious and sacred commitment. One to be taken with care.

Sam wasn't going to fall in love with her.

And she had to let her love for him go.

The cabin swayed. Like a yo-yo on a string, back and forth. Her stomach lurched, but she'd be okay. She knew Sam could handle any turbulence. She wasn't worried about him, but then she did remember the accident. The sensation of falling out of the sky—

Don't think about it. She squeezed her eyes shut along with those old memories.

Then light burned behind her eyelids. The sky rocked with thunder. It's only a bad storm, she thought, but she put her book away and held on to her seat with both hands. They were safe. They were fine.

Lightning flashed, thunder rattled like breaking metal. Kirby bowed her head and started to pray, in case Sam could use a little help. She didn't want anything to go wrong. There was a child in need of a bone marrow transplant, and she was depending on them for her life.

The helicopter dipped hard to the right as Sam banked, and they bounced and swayed in the angry wind.

"Guess that storm is moving faster than those weathermen predicted," he said. "Hold on, it's gonna get rough," he called out. "Don't you worry. This kind of flying is fun for me."

"Fun?" It was a comfort to know he hadn't lost his sense of humor. She was grateful for the seat harness pinning her into the seat as the entire helicopter rose and fell like a child's top. The crash had been like this, the same wild sweeps of movement, the falling...

Please see us through this, she prayed. She forced the memories down, blocking out the blood and death and flames. She gripped the seat more tightly.

Sam's a good pilot. He'll keep us safe. The certainty of that thought calmed her even as lightning electrified the night and burned her eyes.

She could vaguely hear Sam muttering to his controls on the other side of the metal panel, talking to his helicopter as if that would make a difference. She couldn't see him, but she knew he was calm. She could hear it in his voice as he handled the situation with his usual unflappable strength.

She wasn't alone, she realized, and she never had been. Not that afternoon when she'd been laughing with her sister one minute and pummeling toward the earth the next. Not after, when she'd woken to feel her sister's arms around her, her older sister who'd covered her with her body before impact. And saved her life. She wasn't alone in the wreckage as she'd tried to save lives with no medical supplies, no bandages, no help and not enough training.

She hadn't been alone in the hospital afterward or through the years that followed. She had her family, her friends, her community. She had Sam.

Who did Sam have? Ruth. His only living relative. He'd come to Montana from a life of impermanence to put down roots. To find community and comfort.

That's why she'd been brought into his life, she realized. And why he was in hers. Life was a hard journey—it was the way life was. There could not be day without night, light without darkness, happiness without pain, peace without trial.

The best part of life wasn't only the journey, but the love found along the way.

It wasn't over between them, she realized, hope taking her to a quiet, steady place as lightning speared toward her and the helicopter absorbed the impact. The frame sparked, the metal beneath her feet burned, the brightness seared her eyes like fire.

Then they were falling and falling. Silent except for Sam's steady talk.

"C'mon, honey, don't stall on me. C'mon, you can do it. That's right, let's restart. C'mon, start, show me you're the best bird in the sky. You can do it, honey, c'mon."

The altimeter was ticking down. Sam kept an eye on it and the flashing light telling him there was no engine power.

Oh, really? As if he needed a light to tell him that. He had ten, twenty seconds at most, and they were gonna land hard. Right in the middle of the Rockies.

Wasn't that just his luck? Why was it, when he was going to crash, it was always in the worst possible place? A stone's throw from an enemy camp. In the middle of a jungle. Over the sharp peaks of the Rocky Mountains.

Okay, he wasn't going to get his rotors going. The stick was tacky and unresponsive, but he put his muscle into it and he got some response. Enough to mean he'd miss a direct hit to the jagged peak of the mountain. He put his weight on it and prayed for a little more slope. Then he'd catch some cushion, maybe even get the blades turning enough to slow their fall....

Okay, God, a little more help, he prayed, working by rote. He loved the military, bless 'em, for their training. He didn't have to think as he radioed in his distress, his position and shouted for Kirby to make sure she was belted in and to put her head down. They were going to hit. She'd better be alive when this was over, or he'd have a few choice words to give St. Peter when he saw him.

Sam knew he needed his nose down, but the stick was locked up tight. *C'mon, help me out here, just a little. That's all.* He wasn't going to let Kirby down.

He gritted his teeth, put all his weight and strength into it and the locked, rigid stick gave a fraction of an inch. That's it! C'mon, keep going, a little more—

The chopper tipped forward. He saw the ponderosa pine branches a second before glass shattered. Pain exploded in his face, in his chest. His last thought was *I did it*.

He'd made sure he took first impact. Kirby had a chance to survive. That was all that mattered, he thought as darkness swallowed him and, for the first time in his life, he felt real love. Deep love.

Pure. Bright. Perfect.

He'd found his heart. Every piece of it.

Chapter Fourteen

Kirby was certain someone was hitting her on the head with a sledgehammer. She recognized the signs of a concussion—blurry vision, disorientation, dizziness—but fought her way out of the seat harness. Sam.

She stumbled upright, but realized the entire helicopter, broken and crushed as it was, was in one piece and tilting forward. What remained of the chopper was wedged into the cradle of old-growth pines, and the nose was crushed. All she could see was the broken earth where the front of the craft had hit and shattered.

Sam. She scrambled out of her harness, wincing as her ribs ached. Dazed, she struggled over broken branches and pieces of glass and metal. She could only stare. The front of the helicopter—the glass, the controls, the seats—was gone. She smelled fuel and blood and pine sap.

Where was Sam? Panic clawed through her. He was dead. She knew he was. Was he gone? Grief struck her like a fatal blow. She dropped to her knees, trying to hold on. She had to find him. Maybe he'd survived, and if he had, he'd need medical help. He'd need her.

No, this couldn't happen to her twice in a lifetime. She couldn't lose someone she loved like this.

Shaking from shock, she climbed through sheets of crumpled and torn metal. She lost her balance, slid off a branch and landed hard on the ground.

Sam. His body was propped against the tree. As if he'd taken one step and had sunk to the ground. Blood was everywhere. Lord, she needed strength. Enough to handle Sam's death. Enough to save him if she could.

And if she couldn't? Then the strength to comfort him.

He didn't move as she dropped to her knees at his side. His eyes were closed, his head slumped to one side. He didn't appear to be breathing.

Focus, Kirby. Assess the situation. Was he

alive? Her hand trembled as she laid two fingers on his wrist. Joy surged through her at the faint pulse of his beating heart.

Grateful. So grateful. Tears filled her eyes as she went to work. Head trauma. Lacerations. She had to rule out spine injuries and internal bleeding.

His eyes opened. He was conscious. Relief left her spinning, dizzy.

"You're a sight for sore eyes." He held out a bloody hand, trembling, and took hers. "Thank God you're safe."

She held on to him so tight. Couldn't believe he was really there. Alive. He was really alive. "Sam."

His arms wrapped around her. Holding her, holding on. She was so thankful to be here, tucked safe against his chest, where she'd never thought she would be again.

"I can't believe this. You're alive? You're alive." She touched his face, his chest, just to make sure. Her head was hurting too much to think clearly. "I don't believe this. This isn't possible."

"Sure it is." He brushed her tangled hair from her face. "I told you I was pretty good at crashing. You're hurt."

"I'm fine."

"You're bleeding."

"Nothing serious. Not like you."

"Oh, Kirby." His heart broke. Nothing in his life, not his time in the army, not Carla's death, nothing hurt like seeing the blood on her face, the wound bleeding in her scalp and knowing he could have lost her.

He'd been sure he had. He'd thought he was a dead man. He thought he'd never set eyes on her again. He'd known he'd never again hear the music of her voice, see the beauty of her smile, or know the sweetness of her touch. Of her love.

She was alive and safe, and he was so grateful.

Sam had found his heart. He felt the love in it. He loved her. With the strength and integrity of the man he was. To the depth of his soul. Forever.

She withdrew and studied his lacerations, his injuries. Her brow wrinkled with deep worry. "I'm surprised to see you sitting around on the job, Captain."

"It's my nature. I sit around a lot. Moss grows on me."

"Me, too." Kirby studied him, tried to figure out what she needed to do first. Could Sam move? What about spinal injuries? Internal injuries?

She touched his cheek tenderly, careful of the lacerations. He needed her comfort. He needed to know she loved him and he wasn't alone. "I'm writing to customer service. I intend to complain about that landing."

Instead of smiling, the way she'd hoped, his brows furrowed together, as if he was trying to focus, too. "You're bleeding."

"You've already said that."

"I should have done a better job. I'm sorry."

"For what? You kept us alive—that's better than most pilots can do." She brushed a kiss to his forehead, just beneath his hairline. His hair was sticky and dark with blood.

Was the medical equipment on board salvageable? She needed it. If there was internal bleeding—

"Hey, Florence Nightingale, where are you going?" He caught her wrist, holding her when she tried to stand. "You're not climbing back in there. Give me another minute to catch my breath and get on my feet, and I'll do it for you."

"You're injured."

"So are you." He found the strength to pull

her down to her knees. "What about you? You're limping. Zip that coat, will ya? And just sit here. I've got GPS on board. They know we went down, and they know where we are, but it may take a while. We stay warm and alive until they get here, okay?"

"I'm holding you to that." She dimly realized that it was raining. Cold, hard rain that wasn't rain at all. It was snow. In May?

They were in the peaks of the Rockies, she remembered. Where snow stayed until midsummer. Sam was injured, and they had to worry about shock, hypothermia—a thousand different worries flashed into her mind.

"Don't worry, I'm the ranking officer in this crew, and I know what to do." He kissed her cheek. Still commanding, still the same old wonderful Sam. "Let's see your arms. Anything broken?"

"No. I told you, I'm fine. My leg hurts, and my back is sore, but just a little. No traveling pain, no numbness, no weakness. I'm okay. Can you say the same?"

He rolled his eyes. "I'm tough. I don't admit to pain. And speaking of pain, I think my head is starting to clear. Let's see if I can stand without getting sick."

"Sam, you need to rest." She thought of all

the ways he could be injured. Of all the ways she could still lose him.

"I'm gonna be fine." He stood, shaky, but he was a big man, a strong man. He limped as he walked over to stare at what remained of his helicopter. "Wow. Good thing I sprang for the extra insurance."

"Good, because I'm going to sue the company for its choice of unfit pilots."

"Oh, yeah? Well, what are you going to do to the pilot who saves your life? Who has the training it takes to keep you from freezing to death overnight?" He swiped the blood out of his eyes, looking tough and vulnerable, invincible and wounded. And strong. So very strong.

The love she held in her heart for him bubbled over until her eyes teared. How many chances did a person get in life? If she was ever going to learn her lesson, this was it. She'd done her best for her sister and loved her until the end. Loved her still. Sometimes all a person could do was their very best.

Sam was right. How many times would she have to fall out of the sky to accept it? Love was all we had to count on. And in the end, it was all that mattered.

The first chance she could, she was going

to tell Sam what he meant to her. If he didn't like it, too bad. She needed him. She loved him.

And she prayed he felt that way, too.

Watching Kirby work alongside him made Sam more certain than ever. Kirby McKaslin was one in a million. She'd tended his wounds, bandaged his cuts and splinted his left knee and thigh with merciful care. The gentle ministrations, her healing hands, her loving concern stayed with him even as the storm worsened, the snow thickened and the night grew dangerously cold.

"I think I have enough dry branches." Kirby, her hands scratched from the rough work, piled the small brittle limbs in the corner of the shelter.

He'd managed to saw enough bigger pine branches to make a shelter of sorts from what he'd been able to salvage. The dense foliage would keep them dry. Hypothermia was a real threat as the temperature plummeted.

"It won't keep us toasty, but it will keep us from freezing." He held the branch aside that served as a door, and let her in first. "Get comfortable. I've got a few more supplies to fetch, and then we'll stay in for the night."

He'd made them a snug nest of pine and fir branches. And while the cold damp of the earth made her shiver, the small shelter was smartly made.

Leave it to Sam. Was there anything he couldn't do? He was remarkable. He didn't seem aware of it. She took one of the blankets he'd scavenged from the wreckage and wrapped up in it. She was cold, exhausted and shaking. She was in pain.

Don't think about it. Sam's hurt much worse than you are. She could hear him moving outside. What was taking him so long? She worried about him. He might be more hurt than he was saying. She could have lost him tonight, and she wanted him close.

The long thick limbs rustled as Sam shoved them aside to climb into their snug den. The flashlight strapped overhead shadowed him as he hauled in a duffel bag, a plastic container the size of a shoe box and a flare gun. "In case we hear rescue planes," he told her.

He was covered with snow. His teeth chattered as he closed the entrance behind him. "Are you warm yet?"

"Toasty." She shivered, but she smiled.

"Me, too. I found my bag. I have a pair

of sweats we can share. Do you want the bottoms?"

"Yeah." They would fit over her jeans. She accepted the soft thick garment and pulled them on over her tennis shoes. "Got anything to eat in there?"

"Well, I always keep an emergency pack. Let's see what I've got." He snapped open the plastic lid and handed her a packet of beef jerky. "I've got granola bars for breakfast. And an entire pound of chocolate candies."

"You put chocolate in your emergency pack?"

"A day without chocolate is an emergency." Sam stole a stick of jerky from the package she held. "I've got soda, too. We'll have enough to last. Now, bundle up."

"Do you know how amazing you are?" She couldn't help it. She couldn't keep her feelings hidden any longer. And why should she? Life was too short. Too much of a gift. "You can handle anything, can't you?"

"I have my faults, like anyone else." He took a bite of jerky and chewed while he handed her a small silver package. It unfolded into a thermal survival blanket.

Perfect. Sam *could* do anything. Kirby's

regard for him felt as high as heaven and as infinite.

"Come closer. We have to keep you warm." He took her hand and helped cover her with the blanket before he unfolded his own.

With her body heat trapped by the blanket Kirby began feeling less frozen.

"Feel good?" He moved closer and placed his hand on her back. He began to stroke in slow, even caresses that made her hurting spine sing with relief.

Good? She felt fantastic. Well, she was cold and a dull pain was settling into her middle and her head was killing her, but she had Sam. Precious, wonderful Sam. "We should have died tonight. You know that."

"Like I said, I'm pretty good at crashing."

"Yes." She traced the strong, confident angle of his nose with her fingertips. The sparse cut of his lips. The indomitable cut of his jaw. Tenderness filled her, as warm and as sweet as honey, and she pressed a kiss to his cheek.

"Do you know how much I love you?" she said. Just like that, with her heart racing and her fingers trembling and everything at risk.

His eyes widened. Probably with fear.

"Oh, I know what you said tonight. And

I know why you said it." She wasn't going to back down. "You don't want to remarry. You don't want to risk loving anyone again. I understand that. But you could have died tonight. And if you had, then you would have left this earth without knowing how deeply I love you."

"Kirby, look, I can't let you—"

"No, I could have died tonight without telling you how I feel. I need to say this. You are the one man I never thought I'd find. The love I never thought I could deserve. You move my soul like nothing else, and I love you deeply and truly, more than anything on this earth. And I always will."

He closed his eyes. Covered his face with his hands. Rested his elbows on his knees. He looked tortured.

She placed her hand at his nape, at the wide strong column of his neck. She could feel the warm life of him, the give of flesh and muscle and the hard column of his vertebrae. He was so strong.

And as fragile, just like anyone.

"Nothing will ever change how I love you. Even if you don't want me. I'm not like Carla. My feelings for you are real and unbreakable.

You could have died tonight without knowing how deeply you are loved."

"Shhh…" He couldn't take any more. He pulled away, feeling as if she'd reached through his ribs and pulled out his heart, his soul. There was nothing left inside him.

"You don't know what you're saying." It couldn't be true. He wouldn't let it be.

"Yes, I do. I'm not the dimmest bulb in the pack."

It *wasn't* true. It couldn't be. When a woman as good and as incredible as Kirby said words like that to him, she probably had a concussion, because she couldn't mean it. Or maybe it was the situation, the emotion of surviving a second crash, being grateful she was alive and clinging to him. It was the situation. That's what it was.

Her arms came around him from behind, and she laid her cheek against his shoulder blade. Her touch was a love he'd never felt before.

It did match his love for her. Bright. Rare. Terrifying.

How could someone so good be meant for him? He'd been lost for so long, and given up on the hope that there could be happiness for him. Happiness of any kind. So he'd settled for contentment, as lonely as that was.

How did he explain to Kirby that she had to be wrong? That happily-ever-afters were not his experience in life. That he'd learned the hard way that if it looked too good to be true, it was.

No matter how much he wanted it. He turned, slanted his lips over hers and kissed her tenderly. He broke away, knowing he would just end up hurting her. But what other choice did he have? He loved her with a fierceness that felt like pain. Needed her with every drop of his being.

But how could he reach out for a dream? Dreams were only that, illusion and fantasy. He didn't want to survive another fall.

The *whop-whop* of chopper blades had him grabbing the flare gun and diving through the side of the shelter. It was too much to hope it was someone for them. When the bird circled, Sam ran full out, ignoring the pain and the femur he figured was cracked, and made it to the edge of a small clearing. Careful to aim, he pulled the trigger and the flare lit up like a beacon.

They were going home.

But to what? Sam watched Kirby limp

toward him, haloed by the glow of the red flare on the falling snow. She was ashen, walking slowly, fighting pain.

She's hurt worse than she knows, he realized. Worse than he'd thought. She wrapped her arms around her middle, as if doing her best to keep standing. "Did they see us?"

As an answer, the chopper circled wide.

Kirby dropped to her knees. He caught her before she hit the hard-packed snow. The chopper was landing, but all he saw was Kirby. Fighting to stay conscious.

"I'm okay. Really," she insisted, struggling to lift her head from his shoulder.

"Lie still. Shhh." He kissed her brow, holding her tight, a precious weight in his arms.

"Sam!" John Corey, the town's fire chief, reached him first. "Didn't think we'd find you alive. What a godsend. Is she—"

Sam nodded. "She's going into shock. You got an EMT with you?"

"Let's get her in." John and a man who looked way too young to know what he was doing lifted Kirby from Sam's arms.

He had to let her go. He trusted them. He knew she needed them. But he wanted to be the one who held her safe and forever.

John carried her away and into the chopper.

"What about you?" another rescue worker asked.

"Forget about me. She's all that matters."

What had she said to him? *You move my soul like nothing else, and I love you deeply and truly, more than anything on this earth. And I always will.*

That's how he loved her, too. A flawless love that would never end.

What if he lost her? What if he never had the chance to tell her that he'd found his heart after all?

And it was her.

Chapter Fifteen

Sam elbowed open the door to the gift shop with his free hand. Careful of the vase he carried and his left leg's lightweight cast, he hiked through the hospital lobby and took a ride in the elevator to the fifth floor, silently cursing the closemouthed nursing staff as he went.

She's stable, was all they would tell him.

After they'd flown in on the chopper, he'd sat in the waiting area because they made him. There was no room for him while they worked on Kirby. Didn't that make him imagine the worst? She went into surgery to pin a fracture in her lower leg.

Was she awake? In pain? How badly was she hurt? Did she need him? He'd sat there, scared to death, until Jeremiah had hauled

him into a treatment room and forced him to
have his injuries x-rayed. The doc wouldn't
tell him more because Sam wasn't family.
Determined to fix that little problem, Sam
had left the hospital for a quick errand. Now
with a package in his pocket and flowers in
hand, he was going to find her and no one was
going to stop him.

Sam slowed down when he caught sight
of the waiting area on the fifth floor. It was
packed with people of different ages, some
pale with worry, others talking to fill the
silence. The tense worry was palpable as he
came to an abrupt halt in the middle of the
corridor.

The McKaslins. He recognized several of
the sisters as the ones who played Monopoly
with Kirby. There were others who had to
be cousins, older folks who were parents and
uncles and grandparents. An entire family
come together.

This wasn't in his game plan. He hadn't
figured the whole of the McKaslin clan would
rally around Kirby. He'd been shortsighted. He
hadn't considered what having a real family
meant. Kirby had everyone she needed and
loved.

Did she need him?

He was nothing but a banged-up chopper pilot, a veteran with a few medals and too many bad memories that troubled him now and then. He had his failures and his flaws, and that made him all wrong for Kirby.

His hopes sank as he studied the family gathered together. All the well-dressed, perfect and proper folks, who might not consider him the right choice for their golden Kirby.

The question was, did he retreat or did he fight?

Sam Gardner was no coward. There wasn't a battle he hadn't won. He fought to win. And from the moment he'd felt the explosion of the crash and figured he was dead, he'd known beyond a doubt how deep and strong his love went.

To the bottom of his soul. He loved Kirby with all the depth of his being.

"Sam? There you are." The doc—Jeremiah—approached in a white coat, glancing over his shoulder at the McKaslin clan. "Kirby's asking for you."

That had to be good news, right? Determination renewed him. Turned him into steel as he followed the doc down the hall. She wanted him. That was all he needed to know.

"They called in another flight out of Great

Falls. The last I heard little Sarah was safely en route. The procedure's going to save her life." Jeremiah stopped. "This is Kirby's room."

Why was he so nervous? Well, he couldn't stand in the hall all day. He might as well get it over with. Walk in there and tell her how he felt. He was a man. He had a reasonable command of the English language. There was nothing stopping him.

He pushed open the door.

She knew it was him. She didn't have to open her eyes. The halting limp padding across the room was different, but the authoritative power of it was pure Sam. He filled the room with his strength. He filled her heart with an unquenchable light.

"Look who I've got here." The scent of roses filled the air and his footsteps stopped beside her. His fingertips grazed the curve of her face. "Sleeping Beauty. If I kiss her, will she wake?"

His breath was a warm tickle against her cheek. His kiss felt like eternity, like reverence. She opened her eyes. How good it was to see him towering over her, alive and banged up—but he looked whole. Too good to be true.

He had woken her up to her life. The need she felt for Sam came not out of neglect and pain from her past, but out of the newly born places in her soul. Places that had not been alive until Sam knelt at her side and took her hand.

"My very own princess." He swept the bangs out of her eyes, his fingers quaking, his eyes bright with love. "For a while there, I didn't think we'd wind up happily-ever-after."

"You don't believe in happy endings."

"Oh, baby, I do. They're rare. Rare and precious, just like you."

Kirby blinked. The painkillers were making her woozy. Had she heard him right? Had Sam, who'd said he'd never remarry, who was too wounded to try to love again, had he just said—

Her thoughts skidded to a stop at the sight of the black velvet box in the palm of his trembling hand. A ring box. Sam had bought her a ring? Did that mean he wanted her? That he loved her? That this man so good and honorable loved her? Any way. Just the way she was.

"I told you I'd lost my heart." His free hand caught her chin. His gaze pinned hers and she could see into his soul. Into his endless love for her. "I found it. There's a question I've gotta ask you."

He opened the lid. A two-carat diamond sparkled happily on its bed of black velvet. A solitary diamond in a heart cut. The gem glittered with bright prisms of light.

Like the love inside her.

"I love you more than words can say." He lifted the ring from its nest and took her hand. Her left hand. "I can only pray you feel the same way about me. Will you marry me?"

"It would be my honor."

Sam had never heard more beautiful words. He slid the band of gold down the length of her ring finger, so perfect, just like the rest of her. She was his everything. The woman he'd thought he'd never find. For all his hardship and loss in this world, he'd been given back peace and love in greater measure. And it was her.

It was his Kirby.

He'd love her forever. He'd be faithful until his dying day. He would cherish her with every fiber of his being. And she knew it, he realized as he rubbed a tear from her cheek.

The warm wetness skidded across the pad of his thumb, followed by more.

"I love you so much," she confessed.

"I love you too, baby."

He enveloped her in a sweet, tender kiss and Kirby felt ready to break apart with happiness. He crawled in beside her and cradled her carefully against his chest. His arms banded her like steel.

This strong, protective, good-hearted man was all hers forever and ever. Her soul mate. Her most precious gift. Life's gifts were sweet, Kirby discovered, and the greatest of them *was* love.

Epilogue

Two months later

"The bride looks like she could use a cold drink." Michelle stepped around the corner of the espresso machine set up on the roomy back porch and held out an iced mocha with extra whipped cream. "Just as you like it."

"You're a lifesaver. Thanks." Kirby shifted the veil—it kept tumbling over her shoulder and getting in the way—and took a deep gulp of the icy drink. When she'd hoped for a beautiful July day for her wedding, she hadn't known the angels had taken her wish to heart.

Where had Sam gone? He'd been caught in a huddle with her cousin, her uncles and her grandfather discussing their military experiences. But she didn't see him in the backyard, where tables had been set up around the gazebo Sam had built for her. Where they'd married beneath an arbor of climbing roses.

"It was a beautiful ceremony, dear." Ruth sidled close to select several mints from the candy dish. "And the cake was delicious. I must say, it's good to see Sam happy again. I prayed this day would come."

Kirby gave her new aunt a hug. "I'm so glad you've decided to move in next door to us."

"I was surprised Sam offered. The big house was getting too much for me, and I'm getting older. It will be a comfort to know you kids are right next door, if I should be in need. What a blessing you are, my dear. Now, you go find that husband of yours. I think he was looking for you."

"Where did you see him?"

"In the kitchen with the dogs. Goodness knows where he is now."

Kirby slipped past her mom and her gramma, who tried to hail her down to talk. She'd get back to them. She tingled with the need to see her husband. They'd been married only one hour and ten minutes, but she knew their life together was going to be a joy. How could it not be? She'd married her one true love.

"Hey, sis." Karen was sitting at the kitchen table, nursing newborn Allison. "If you're looking for your husband, he went out front with the dogs."

"Thanks." Kirby hurried through the living room around the two recliners Sam had moved in just this morning, and onto the front porch.

Sam. Her heart rose when she saw him. As it always did. As it always would.

As if he could feel her presence, he turned. "Hey, beautiful. Who's the lucky guy?"

"Just some man I settled for." She lifted the lace skirt and tapped down the steps in her satin ballet slippers. "I figure the marriage will last two weeks, tops. But you know how desperate we women of a certain age are."

"Boy, do I. It's shocking how you threw yourself at me." Sam hurled the orange bone along the length of the front yard, and both Leo and Jessie took off in a mad dash after it. "That will keep them busy. Come here,

Mrs. Gardner. I have something for you. My everlasting love, and this is just the start."

He wrapped her in his arms, and his kiss was long and sweet.

* * * * *

LARGER-PRINT BOOKS!

**GET 2 FREE
LARGER-PRINT NOVELS
PLUS 2 FREE
MYSTERY GIFTS**

Larger-print novels are now available...

YES! Please send me 2 FREE LARGER-PRINT Love Inspired® novels and my 2 FREE mystery gifts (gifts are worth about $10). After receiving them, if I don't wish to receive any more books, I can return the shipping statement marked "cancel". If I don't cancel, I will receive 6 brand-new novels every month and be billed just $4.74 per book in the U.S. or $5.24 per book in Canada. That's a saving of at least 24% off the cover price. It's quite a bargain! Shipping and handling is just 50¢ per book in the U.S. and 75¢ per book in Canada.* I understand that accepting the 2 free books and gifts places me under no obligation to buy anything. I can always return a shipment and cancel at any time. Even if I never buy another book, the two free books and gifts are mine to keep forever.

122/322 IDN FC79

Name   (PLEASE PRINT)

Address   Apt. #

City   State/Prov.   Zip/Postal Code

Signature (if under 18, a parent or guardian must sign)

Mail to the **Reader Service:**
IN U.S.A.: P.O. Box 1867, Buffalo, NY 14240-1867
IN CANADA: P.O. Box 609, Fort Erie, Ontario L2A 5X3

Not valid to current subscribers to Love Inspired Larger-Print books.

**Are you a current subscriber to Love Inspired books
and want to receive the larger-print edition?
Call 1-800-873-8635 or visit www.ReaderService.com.**

LILPII

LARGER-PRINT BOOKS!

**GET 2 FREE
LARGER-PRINT NOVELS
PLUS 2 FREE
MYSTERY GIFTS**

Love Inspired®

SUSPENSE
RIVETING INSPIRATIONAL ROMANCE

Larger-print novels are now available...

YES! Please send me 2 FREE LARGER-PRINT Love Inspired® Suspense novels and my 2 FREE mystery gifts (gifts are worth about $10). After receiving them, if I don't wish to receive any more books, I can return the shipping statement marked "cancel". If I don't cancel, I will receive 4 brand-new novels every month and be billed just $4.74 per book in the U.S. or $5.24 per book in Canada. That's a saving of at least 24% off the cover price. It's quite a bargain! Shipping and handling is just 50¢ per book in the U.S. and 75¢ per book in Canada.* I understand that accepting the 2 free books and gifts places me under no obligation to buy anything. I can always return a shipment and cancel at any time. Even if I never buy another book, the two free books and gifts are mine to keep forever.

110/310 IDN FC7L

Name	(PLEASE PRINT)	
Address		Apt. #
City	State/Prov.	Zip/Postal Code

Signature (if under 18, a parent or guardian must sign)

Mail to the **Reader Service:**
IN U.S.A.: P.O. Box 1867, Buffalo, NY 14240-1867
IN CANADA: P.O. Box 609, Fort Erie, Ontario L2A 5X3

Not valid for current subscribers to Love Inspired Suspense larger-print books.

**Are you a current subscriber to Love Inspired Suspense books
and want to receive the larger-print edition?
Call 1-800-873-8635 or visit www.ReaderService.com.**

* Terms and prices subject to change without notice. Prices do not include applicable taxes. Sales tax applicable in N.Y. Canadian residents will be charged applicable taxes. Offer not valid in Quebec. This offer is limited to one order per household. All orders subject to credit approval. Credit or debit balances in a customer's account(s) may be offset by any other outstanding balance owed by or to the customer. Please allow 4 to 6 weeks for delivery. Offer available while quantities last.

Your Privacy—The Reader Service is committed to protecting your privacy. Our Privacy Policy is available online at www.ReaderService.com or upon request from the Reader Service.

We make a portion of our mailing list available to reputable third parties that offer products we believe may interest you. If you prefer that we not exchange your name with third parties, or if you wish to clarify or modify your communication preferences, please visit us at www.ReaderService.com/consumerschoice or write to us at Reader Service Preference Service, P.O. Box 9062, Buffalo, NY 14269. Include your complete name and address.

LISUSLP11

REQUEST YOUR FREE BOOKS!

2 FREE INSPIRATIONAL NOVELS
PLUS 2
FREE
MYSTERY GIFTS

Love Inspired
HISTORICAL
INSPIRATIONAL HISTORICAL ROMANCE

YES! Please send me 2 FREE Love Inspired® Historical novels and my 2 FREE mystery gifts (gifts are worth about $10). After receiving them, if I don't wish to receive any more books, I can return the shipping statement marked "cancel". If I don't cancel, I will receive 4 brand-new novels every month and be billed just $4.24 per book in the U.S. or $4.74 per book in Canada. That's a saving of at least 23% off the cover price. It's quite a bargain! Shipping and handling is just 50¢ per book in the U.S. and 75¢ per book in Canada.* I understand that accepting the 2 free books and gifts places me under no obligation to buy anything. I can always return a shipment and cancel at any time. Even if I never buy another book, the two free books and gifts are mine to keep forever.

102/302 IDN FDCH

Name	(PLEASE PRINT)
Address	Apt. #
City	State/Prov.	Zip/Postal Code

Signature (if under 18, a parent or guardian must sign)

Mail to the **Reader Service:**
IN U.S.A.: P.O. Box 1867, Buffalo, NY 14240-1867
IN CANADA: P.O. Box 609, Fort Erie, Ontario L2A 5X3

Not valid for current subscribers to Love Inspired Historical books.

Want to try two free books from another series?
Call 1-800-873-8635 or visit www.ReaderService.com.

---

* Terms and prices subject to change without notice. Prices do not include applicable taxes. Sales tax applicable in N.Y. Canadian residents will be charged applicable taxes. Offer not valid in Quebec. This offer is limited to one order per household. All orders subject to credit approval. Credit or debit balances in a customer's account(s) may be offset by any other outstanding balance owed by or to the customer. Please allow 4 to 6 weeks for delivery. Offer available while quantities last.

Your Privacy—The Reader Service is committed to protecting your privacy. Our Privacy Policy is available online at www.ReaderService.com or upon request from the Reader Service.

We make a portion of our mailing list available to reputable third parties that offer products we believe may interest you. If you prefer that we not exchange your name with third parties, or if you wish to clarify or modify your communication preferences, please visit us at www.ReaderService.com/consumerchoice or write to us at Reader Service Preference Service, P.O. Box 9062, Buffalo, NY 14269. Include your complete name and address.

LIH11

Harlequin®

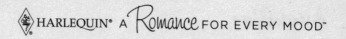

HARLEQUIN® A *Romance* FOR EVERY MOOD™

From passion, paranormal, suspense and
adventure, to home and family,
Harlequin has a romance for everyone!

Visit

www.TryHarlequin.com/BOOKS

to choose from a variety of
great series romance stories
that are absolutely FREE to download!

(Total approximate retail value $60.)

Look for all the variety Harlequin has to offer
wherever books are sold, including
most bookstores, supermarkets,
discount stores and drugstores.

Love Inspired®
SUSPENSE
RIVETING INSPIRATIONAL ROMANCE

Watch for our series of edge-
of-your-seat suspense novels.
These contemporary tales
of intrigue and romance
feature Christian characters
facing challenges to their faith...
and their lives!

AVAILABLE IN REGULAR
& LARGER-PRINT FORMATS

Love Inspired.
HISTORICAL
INSPIRATIONAL HISTORICAL ROMANCE

Engaging stories of romance,
adventure and faith,
these novels are set in
various historical periods
from biblical times
to World War II.

NOW AVAILABLE!